The Seven Year

Dress

A Novel

PAULETTE MAHURIN

ISBN: 978-0-9888468-6-9

Published by Early Girl Enterprises, LLC

Printed in the United States of America

For my father and mother, their siblings, and all the children

Other books by Paulette Mahurin

The Persecution of Mildred Dunlap

His Name Was Ben

To Live Out Loud

Acknowledgment

To my talented critical readers, Carol and Lee, a heartfelt thank you.

To my incredibly detail-oriented, brilliant editor, Dr. L. Lee, this book would not be possible without you. And to the publishing house of Early Girl Enterprises, thank you for believing in Helen's story and helping her voice reach the world.

To the love of my life, words truly fail me when I say I couldn't have done this without you, my hubby and my best friend. You were there with your support, kindness, back and foot rubs, prepared meals, millions of read-throughs and feedback, and unconditional love. You are positively the best!

To all those who endured the unthinkable intolerance and persecution because of your bloodline, you will not be forgotten.

Finally, to Helen, who graciously rented me a room and, in that small apartment, opened me to an understanding and compassion I never knew possible. You are forever in my heart, my dear friend.

The Seven Year Dress

Everything can be taken from a man but one thing:

the last of human freedoms - to choose one's attitude in

any given set of circumstances, to choose one's own

way.

Viktor E. Frankl

The Seven Year Dress

Foreword

Although this story is a historical fiction, much of what you will read is documented historical fact about the Jewish holocaust in the 20th century. Many of the scenes and the content in the narrative have been taken from historical references. Creative liberties were taken when fact mingled with fiction to create a coherent, fluid narrative that remained true to this compelling moment in time and to those people who were a part of it. Such was the case with the lovemaking scenes in Auschwitz. I felt that it was important to include that human needs and drives, natural to all of us, were not extinguished in some of the prisoners enduring the atrocities. It was with dignity and respect that I endeavored to depict the men, women, and children who suffered the torturous, unthinkable conditions of Hitler's pogrom.

The real Helen Stein bestowed upon me a gift of compassion and humility in sharing her story with me. In telling this story, I hope I serve her well.

Prologue

Present Day

I was looking to rent a room. She was looking for family. I needed a place to live. She needed to fill an empty void in her heart. But it would take me a few weeks to realize the role I was to play in her life.

She appeared old and worn out, years of a hard life etched on her dry, chapped, and pale skin. She had a restrained desperation about her that gave me pause, a niggling feeling that something about her was terribly wrong. Keeping me at her front door for an unusually long time, she asked me a lot of personal questions, like was I working, and could she trust me to pay the rent. *Trust me?* I thought it odd and wondered if she had mental problems.

My college classes were starting the next week, and I needed to find an affordable room. I'm a private person and her interrogation made me feel ill at ease. Had I not been under so much pressure, I would have turned around and walked away. Walked away from this strange shriveled person. But I didn't have time to listen to my gut. Hoping I wouldn't regret it, I answered her questions and walked through her doorway.

Her apartment was musty and dark. But it was neat. Pristine. Oddly, it helped me relax to see everything in its proper place, aligned with what looked like well-thought-out spaces between objects, fastidious appearing. Her attention to detail fascinated me, but, because of her manner moments earlier, I became anxious again, wondering if she was an obsessive-compulsive personality. *What the hell am I getting myself into?*

"Would you a like a tea?"

A tea? Not, would you like a cup of tea? "No thank you. I don't have much time right now. Could I see the room you have for rent?"

"I need to ask you a few more questions first," she said.

It occurred to me we hadn't spoken our names. I knew hers from an earlier phone conversation, and she knew mine. But so far our interaction involved only questions.

"Where do you live now?"

"I'm sharing a room with a girl who is moving to go to graduate school on the East Coast."

"I'm assuming you can't afford to live there alone?"

"Correct," I answered.

"And you don't want to look for another roommate there?"

Oh man, what's with all these questions? "I don't have time to advertise. It was easier to look for another room to rent."

When she nodded her head, indicating she appeared satisfied with my answer, she asked, "Do you have family?"

Where the hell is this going? "Yes, I—"

She interrupted me to ask, "Are your parents alive?"

My skin began to itch and I picked at a fingernail. I had second thoughts. *Should I chuck this all in?* "Yes." I squirmed in my seat. "I don't mean to be rude, but I'd really like to know if you'll rent me the room? I'm up against a time—"

"Are you Jewish?" she interjected.

What does this have to do with renting a room? Just as I was about to beg off, I saw tears welling in her eyes. Her

3

sorrowful expression gave me pause. *She wants to know if I'm Jewish.* Something changed in her when she asked me that. And that something was undeniable.

Although raised by Jewish parents who were moderately religious, I never observed the religion. I defined myself as an agnostic. Questioning the intangible began when my close friend was brutally murdered at an early age. A robber killed her in her own house. Compounding the shock and terror I felt at losing my friend so suddenly and violently, I was gripped with fear of being in my own home because this horrible crime happened next door. To this day, religion provides me no solace and no answers for why innocent people get killed, especially children.

She was waiting for an answer about my beliefs and I didn't want to answer. *Shit!* I couldn't lie and say I'm Jewish. I didn't know a thing about the religion. Plus, my workaholic parents were never around to teach me much of anything. What I learned, I learned from life's experiences, relationships, and formal education. She sat there, patiently waiting for my answer. Finally, I responded, "My parents are Jewish."

She nodded approval. "And you?"

"Helen," finally breaking the ice and referring to her by name, I said, "Please tell me why is this important? I'm not comfortable talking about my beliefs, and I don't want to offend anyone by disagreeing with theirs."

"That is a fair and honest answer." She smiled. The first smile in the forty minutes since we met. "So tell me, Myra, you are a student? Where do you go to school?"

She surprised and relaxed me with her response and the in-kind mention of my name. "UCLA. I'm in the nursing program."

A dark shadow moved over her face as her eyes lost focus. She had moved into some thought that dropped a grim veil over her, a heavy energy into what had just lightened. She shook her head as if to snap out of some nightmare and said, "You see a lot of suffering." She moved her hand to scratch her neck.

"In some of the hospital rotations, yes, I do," I responded.

As her fingers moved along dehydrated ridges on the surface of her parched skin, the sleeve of the sweater she was wearing crept up her arm, and I saw it. A number! My heart sank. I felt ashamed of my I-don't-care-about-you-let's-get-this-over-with attitude. This woman had been in a concentration camp. What horrors had she experienced? No wonder she seemed unusual. Feeling the heaviness she must have lived through, the oddity about this woman started to fall into place when I realized she had been in a concentration camp. And like the moon moves into the night illuminating the darkness, my discomfort drifted away. I wondered what her story was.

With my eyes still on those numbers, I noticed she flushed and quickly pulled her sweater back down to cover the markings. The branding into her flesh at the hands of the vilest evil was done to rob her of her identity, her existence. Now, having seen those numbers, I looked into her eyes and saw a thousand tons of sorrow, an agony I could never imagine with any semblance of veracity. I hadn't understood the glimpse of her apprehension earlier when she asked me if I was Jewish. Now it made sense.

She clutched her hands together and spoke, "Suffering is not just in hospitals." Just when she looked like she wanted to say more, her eyes filled with tears again. And all she said was, "Let me show you the room."

Two days later, with a suitcase, my book bag filled with textbooks, and a few canned goods that I could keep in my room, I moved in. The relatively large room, with a wall-to-wall closet for clothes and storage, had a couch in it that turned into a pull-out bed. Across from the bed was a window that looked down on the street a story below. From that view, I could see Melrose Avenue a few buildings to the north. It was the heart of the Fairfax district in Los Angeles, a Jewish area that was a gentrified, up-beat neighborhood with off-Broadway theaters, antique shops, and many great eateries. Close by was Canter's Deli. Compared to the brightness and colors of outside, mine was a stark room with light beige walls devoid of paintings or ornaments; it had a musty, unlived-in smell.

I opened the window to air out the room, unpacked my clothes, took out my books and placed my canned goods on the desk by the window. Kitchen privileges weren't included in the reduced-rent deal I made with Helen, but I could use the stove to boil water to make instant coffee or tea. I'd eat out of cans or grab take-out. In the hallway adjacent to my room was my bathroom, which faced Helen's bedroom with an en suite bathroom. I was relieved with this privacy. Beside the tiny kitchen, with an adjacent place for a table that sat four, was a small living room: the entire apartment space totaled 900 square feet. Again, like my room, the living room was painted a muted beige and sparsely furnished. Aside from the kitchenette furniture, the living room had two brown, comfy chairs and a small table facing and separating them from a three-seat, faded green couch with rips around the edges of the back pillows. Next to the couch was a tiny end table with a lamp and a couple of indiscernible objects on it that I didn't give much notice to.

During my first night there, I had trouble sleeping. The lumpy bed with visible springs creaked when I moved and dug into my back. A blanket folded under me didn't help. Nor did my restless mind. I couldn't get my attention off of Helen, just a few feet away. *What was it like to sleep in a concentration camp?*

The ticking of the clock held my attention as images of cachectic bodies flashed in my head. Finally after a futile attempt at sleep, at close to three in the morning, sweat drenched, I got up to shake loose the haunting impressions. I walked around her living room looking at her things. My attention went to an aged, brownish-edged doily on the small table that reminded me of my grandma who used to crochet. An aroma of something like onions and chicken, from what she must have prepared for her dinner, lingered in the kitchen. I glanced in there and noticed half-filled jars of raisins, dates, prunes, and dried apples on the kitchen counter, and I thought it odd that they all had the same amount of fruit in them. The exacting neatness gave me a chill. The sparseness of personal items was unsettling, no photos of family members, not one hidden album, and, aside from one store-bought, mass-produced photograph of flowers, her walls were bare. There was nothing that told me about Helen or her past, with one exception, but I had no idea what it meant. It was a faded piece of material in a glass-covered frame that sat on the end table. The tattered swatch of dimly colored blue cotton had a floral print. Little swirls of lighter shades outlined the design of the stained material. My eyes went to a plaque attached to the bottom of the frame that read, *Nothing Lasts*. I couldn't help wondering, *What is this old fabric? And what caused the rust-colored stains splattered on it that look like blood?*

As the weeks passed, I hardly saw Helen. I spent most of my time on campus, in the library or class. On some of the occasions when I did see her, we shared a cup of tea and pleasantries. She was careful not to divulge anything about herself. The more she held back, the more I wanted to help her open up about what had happened to her. I wanted her to trust and confide in me. I wanted to be that safe place she could land if she needed a friend. The part of me that was studying to become a nurse had a need to comfort her. I couldn't help the strong desire I felt to want to go deeper with her. I also couldn't help my curiosity about wanting to know what she had experienced in the concentration camp.

It was long in coming, but finally, one night I came home depressed that a patient I was taking care of had died. Rare as it was for Helen to comment about my feelings, she said, "You don't look too happy."

Knowing she must have experienced unimaginable trauma to have those numbers on her arm, and considering that she never spoke of any family nor had photos, I hesitated to bring up death. "I'm okay," I lied.

She smiled warmly. "Would you like to talk?"

There was something different about this enigmatic woman I'd been living with for the past several months. She had softened. Here I was all these past weeks trying to help her, and it was she who moved our relationship to the deeper personal place I longed for. Surprised and grateful, I responded in kind by opening to her. "It was my first night in the emergency room." Out of respect for Helen's still undisclosed experiences, I refrained from discussing the gruesome details. The fatal gunshot wound to my patient's head was worse than I expected to encounter. "I didn't think it would be so violent."

The unspoken appeared clear to Helen. "Oh, I see." She averted her eyes from mine. "I'm sorry," she mumbled. We both looked down to her hands; they shook as she fidgeted with her dress. *Had I ever seen her in anything but a dress...with soft floral designs? No.*

"I didn't mean to upset you, Helen."

She snapped back up straight and glared at me. "You think that upset me?" Her eyes filled with moisture. "Oh my dear girl, no..."

The proverbial door was open. I could no longer resist. This felt like the right, no, the only, moment. "Perhaps you are the one who needs to talk?" I reached my hand for hers and let her cry. And with those tears, when words failed us, came camaraderie.

"Yes," she wiped the streams of wetness from her cheeks, "I think I do." She reached to the end table with the framed swatch and took it in her hands. "Perhaps a fresh pot of tea, if you wouldn't mind."

While I was in the kitchen heating the water, I heard her moan and weep, "Papa..."

When I returned, she was holding the framed fabric to her breast. While I poured the tea, she looked at me with bloodshot eyes and said, "My Papa told me life is precious. I had to die many times to truly understand this."

Chapter One

Early 1920s

Who could have possibly imagined that in three years a decorated veteran of World War I would become the leader of the National Socialist German Workers' Party, and years later become Chancellor of Germany and annihilate millions of Jews? Certainly not me, Helen Stein. While Hitler was gaining popularity in the German Workers' Party in 1919, I was born to a Jewish family in Berlin. My father, Irving Stein, at thirty-one-years old, was a government lawyer who adored his wife—my mother, Rose—a few years younger than he. Altogether, there were six of us. I was the youngest of the four siblings: Lawrence was seven years older, Shana was five years older, and Ben was four years older than me.

My mother lost a child to a stillbirth before I was born, which made her overly protective of me. When I was old enough to understand, she told me she worried more about me, the baby in the family, because of that loss. I also learned about the impact it had on my father when I overheard him praying one night. Down on his knees I heard him ask God to "watch over all my children. Please, no more losses like our baby Jacob." They named the baby they lost Jacob. To my parents every life was precious, and although they hardly ever spoke of it openly, this was not a loss that easily moved from their consciousness with time. In conversations, in prayer, behind closed doors, the loss of Jacob—and the preciousness of life itself—was something my father and mother reflected on from time to time. I had a bad habit of eavesdropping, which is how I overheard a lot of what went on in privacy.

I came into the world in a time of great turmoil, civil unrest, and economic upheaval in the aftermath of The Great War that took the lives of more than nine million people. Ending the year before I was born, the war sent ripples throughout the countries that were affected, causing massive political, cultural, and social changes. Especially impacted was Germany, where a socialist revolution led to the formulation of a number of communist parties. The Treaty of Versailles (written by the victors, of course) placed blame for the entire war on Germany and levied a fine of 132 billion marks—more than 31 billion dollars—to keep the German economy from flourishing. To honor the restitution, the German Republic printed large amounts money. The economic effect was devastating. Hyperinflation made the German mark near valueless, and Germany fell into default. As a result, German territories were transferred to other countries. Because many Germans never accepted the treaty as legal and viewed the taking of their territories as hostile, the German Workers' Party, later renamed the National Socialist German Workers' Party (NSGWP, referred to in English as the Nazi Party), emerged. Created as a means to draw workers away from communist uprisings, the Party's initial strategy was anti-big business, anti-bourgeois, and anti-capitalism, although these features were later downplayed to get support from industrial organizations. Harboring anti-Semitism from its founding, in the 1930s its focus would change to anti-Semitic and anti-Marxist ideas. I remember my parents talking about those earlier events through the years, but I never understood the foreboding tone in their voices until much later, in late 1938, when all hell broke loose.

But back to when I was growing up. The first national politician to protest and take actions against the treaty's conditions was Adolf Hitler, a move gaining him national support. As the Party grew, my father was employed by the German government to write and negotiate contracts. He worked day and night, remaining a part of a cadre of government lawyers until years later. As Hitler's popularity increased, his oratory propaganda continued to denounce global capitalism and communism as being a component of a Jewish conspiracy. As the rhetoric intensified and hatred grew, my father was removed from his government employment.

In 1921, when I turned two-years-old, Hitler became the leader of the Nazi Party. As I was learning to combine words into simple sentences and took pride in my new accomplishment, the evil voice of the man rising to power was gaining followers. To German citizens flocking to hear him in hopes of employment, Hitler was the illusion and promise of a better life. Little did we know he would be our death sentence.

"Helen, put that down!" My mother scolded me for grabbing a thin glass vase that I was about to insert in my mouth. She ran to remove it from my tiny wet hand. "I cannot turn my back for a minute," she laughed. Picking me up, she gave me a hug and handed me to my sister Shana. "Watch your baby sister." Mamma smiled before turning around and heading to the kitchen. She spent most of her day preparing three meals and cleaning up after our active family. She loved to cook and, thankfully for the rest of us, made delicious meals. She was among the Jews in Berlin that did not keep kosher, which kept her domestic life simpler while tending to us children.

"Mamma that smells so good," my older brother, Lawrence, said. "Is it a chocolate cake?" Shana carried me into the kitchen to watch.

"Yes, Larry." Mamma stirred flour into the wet mix, dripping white fluffs onto the counter.

"For Helen's birthday?" He waited for her to finish and turn her back, before sticking a finger into the batter and then into my mouth. "Big girl's two years old," he said playfully as he painted my forehead.

When she turned to face us, her stern look faded into laughter. They all giggled at the sight of chocolate on my face. "Okay now, out of the kitchen and let me finish my work. Larry, go outside and play with your brother Ben."

While Mamma prepared the festivities, my beloved sister played hide-the-object to entertain me. In front of me, she took a book and hid it, and then she asked me, "Helen, where is it?" I took great satisfaction in slamming my little fist down on the pillow it was under and waited for recognition that I accomplished the task. "Good girl," she patted my back.

I toddled over to another spot on the couch where the pillows were and patted it. "More," I squealed. "Do it again."

The game and playtime went on until my father came home and it was time to celebrate. "Are Ludwig and Ela bringing Max over?" my father asked referring to our neighbors, the Müllers, and their son, who had recently turned two. Both Ela and my mother were pregnant at the same time. Max and I were perfect playmates, poking and prodding one another. Even then, I was his best friend.

As the years passed, Max and I became inseparable. He came to our home for meals, and I went to his. He was an only child, so he especially loved coming over to a warm home filled with noisy fun kids running around, all older than the two of us. Max was particularly fond of my brother Ben, so I was surprised when, in 1929, at the age of ten, he came crying to me that Ben was not nice to him. "What happened?" I asked Max.

"I don't want to talk about it," he pouted.

"You just told me he was mean to you. Tell me the rest." Sitting on a wooden bench in our backyard, I waited several minutes and watched him cry. "Max," I put my hand on his back and felt the heat pouring from his body. "What is it? You can tell me."

His breathing calmed. "He pushed me away."

"What do you mean? What did he do?"

"He changed toward me. He wasn't warm. It was like my friend disappeared."

"Why?" I asked. "What happened?"

Max's face turned red, and his breathing quickened. He shook his bowed head. "I feel ashamed."

"Oh Max, it can't be that bad. Talk to me. You've always been able to talk to me."

"I know, but this is different."

"Max, you're my best friend. It's me, Helen."

Finally, with an agonized wince he said, "He called me a *goy*!"

It wasn't so much the word that shook me, but the way his tone changed when he said it. He was angry. I had never seen Max so upset. My chest tightened painfully, and a heaviness moved between us that had not been there before. My brother Ben was loving and kind. I didn't understand any of this. My parents had shielded me from adult talk about the dark shadows of fear and hatred moving into our city and our country.

Taking in a deep, slow breath, I calmed my nerves. Intuitively, I felt that something awful was entering my life, but I was at a loss for words. How could I get Max to open up about his feelings? Like occasions in the past, I rested in the assurance that, if we talked honestly, all would be well. I wondered if what was happening to Max now was similar to the time he wanted to play with my dolls. I knew that dolls were for girls, but I listened and didn't make fun of him. What he wanted didn't make sense to a little girl, but now I was just a couple of years away from becoming a woman. I was beginning to understand his preference for girl toys, his affection for my brother Ben, and why Ben's comment hurt his feelings.

"I'm sure Ben didn't mean to hurt your feelings."

"Yes, he did!" His shoulders slumped. He looked down at his hands, his chin trembling. Max's moist eyes avoided mine when he continued. "Ben asked me if I had heard the rumors about a man named Hitler." Max then relayed some ugly things that Ben had said to him. He wiped a tear from his cheek. "When I told Ben I thought it was nonsense, he sarcastically said he knew I wouldn't believe it because I'm a…a goy!"

Nausea rose in my belly. I was young, sheltered from the harsh political currents roiling around me, but I was still aware of how important religious beliefs were in defining what and who was acceptable. To me, the fuss seemed silly. Max was Max—my best friend. I didn't care that he was different from me: a boy (who liked girl things), blonde, Christian, an only child. What difference did those differences make? I was confused and frightened for him, but I wanted to help him. Trying to calm him, and myself, I said, "All this political stuff can't be all that serious, Max." But deep inside I knew it was deadly serious.

At my insistence, Max talked with Ben and all was forgiven. For me, that was a wonderful example of how easy it was to solve problems when people have love, not hate, in their hearts. In my family, we grew up to embrace things we liked and not dwell on what we disliked, for one can always find fault in another. I've often felt that we humans are more alike than not, and, if we want to keep the peace, it's not difficult to find something on which to agree.

Later, after that incident with my brother and Max, I learned that this man named Hitler hated Jews. After his attempted coup to seize power in Munich in 1923, Hitler was imprisoned and wrote *Mein Kampf,* which had several passages involving genocide. "The nationalization of our masses will succeed only when, aside from all the positive struggle for the soul of our people, their international poisoners are exterminated," Hitler wrote. He elaborated, "if at the beginning of the War and during the War twelve or fifteen thousand of these Hebrew corrupters of the people had been held under poison gas, as happened to hundreds of thousands of our very best German workers in the field, the sacrifice of millions at the front would not have been in vain." I will never forget the day in the library when I read those words.

Although my parents tried, protecting the family from Hitler's hatred was impossible. His message became a stench in the air that everyone was forced to breathe. Out on the streets groups were forming, for Hitler and against

Jews and other undesirables. The first time I heard the word *undesirable* defined, homosexuality was listed. I thought of Max and his attraction to Ben. His affinity to play with dolls. I couldn't help wondering if Max had also heard those words and was *goy* the only label he feared?

Chapter Two

The day Max finally confided in me that he liked boys changed our relationship and our lives. Years later when Hitler's vengeance against Jews, homosexuals, and others was in full fury, it would be the trust of our shared secret and the closeness that allowed it, that saved my life. The day Max opened up to me was cold and rainy. It mimicked his recently increasing disheartened mood. We were thirteen and I had an awful crush on Isaac Blau, a boy in our school. As Max and I were walking home after the last class, I couldn't contain myself.

"I didn't sleep last night," I giggled.

Max knew me well. Responding to the silliness in my tone, he said, "The Blau boy?"

"Yes," I laughed. "He gave me another look today. He's *so* cute!"

"He *is* cute," Max nudged me in the ribs with his elbow and gave me an exaggerated wink.

I was taken aback by the response, assuming he was mocking me. Pulling a long face, I said, "You're making fun of me."

"Huh?" His voice rose several pitches. He waved his arms in the air. "What? No! Never! I wouldn't...I couldn't do that! Not to you!"

Startled for a moment by the volume and force of his response, I looked around to be sure no one was in earshot. "Then why did you react that way?"

Lowering his voice, he said. "I happen to think he *is* cute."

"What?" My body jerked back.

Max grabbed my shoulders to steady me. "I wasn't joking. And I certainly wasn't making fun of you." He took in a deep slow breath. His eyes softened into loving warmth that eased the tension out of my rigid torso.

Had Max confirmed what I had earlier suspected? I took my time before I spoke. "Max..." I had to know for sure, but I didn't know how to ask him something so personal and so potentially dangerous given the current political situation. "Are you saying what I think you're saying?" He instantly stood erect and his body tightened.

When an embarrassed flush blossomed over his fair skin, I regretted opening my mouth.

He looked down and went silent. The tenderness he expressed seconds earlier dissolved into the atmosphere. Was he too uncomfortable, too afraid, to speak out loud what I believed to be his secret? When his jaw muscles tensed and sweat beaded on his forehead, I lifted his chin to make eye contact. "Max, you're my closest friend. You know everything about me. If you need to confide in me about anything…"

"It's not that easy." Tears dripped from his red face. "I can't."

In that silence, I came to understand that Max and I each had something very real to fear as "undesirables" living in Germany at this moment in history. The difference was that, if he was very smart and lucky, he might be able to pretend that he was not an "undesirable." I was smart, but would never be that lucky. But I could already see the price he paid for concealing his true self. He was guarded and moody, not the sweet Max I grew to love and call my best friend. His secret was eating away at him, but revealing his secret—even to me—could have dire consequences. Many minutes had passed before I took his hand. "Let's go somewhere safe."

I led him to a nearby park, and there, among the birch trees and capercaillie, we sat on an isolated bench. He remained quiet as I watched one of the birds puff up its slate-gray and brown plumage and spread its wings to take flight. Its freedom made me aware of how confined Max must be feeling.

In the privacy of the shaded, remote area, he cried openly. When he finished crying, he blew his nose and laughed.

"What are you laughing at?"

"It's nerves. Anxiety, you know, coming out."

Wanting to make it safe for him to express himself, I said nothing and just smiled.

"I do trust you," he said. "But I don't know that you understand the extent of what is happening in our country." He bit his lower lip and squeezed my hand. Then said, "We're both in danger."

"Oh, Max! You're being overly dramatic." I smiled, referring to his flare for the theatrics.

With humbled, hunched shoulders, he responded, "Not this time, Helen. What's happening in Germany is serious."

He went on to tell me that representatives of the Hitler Youth movement had already contacted him and wanted him to join when he turned fourteen. Boys his age would surround him day and night—boys who probably all liked girls except for him. He would have to pretend to share an interest in girls and a hatred of all "undesirables" while hiding any urges that may develop. If he couldn't manage all of that to be a "good Nazi," he feared the consequences. "And worse," he started to cry again, "I will never be with a boy!"

Max's affirmation broke my heart. Before he cast his eyes to the ground, I saw a depth of sorrow in them that pierced my heart. I put one hand over my chest in a useless attempt to protect myself from all of this pain—mine, his, ours. Max slowly raised his head and continued. "You are the only person in the world I can talk to."

Not knowing what to say, and desperately wanting to comfort him, I asked, "What about your parents? Don't you think they'd want to know?"

"No! It would kill them."

"They love you, Max. You don't know how they would react. Is it your religion?" I was referring to his Catholic upbringing.

"No, they're not overly religious. It's the…" He stopped talking and clenched his fists. "You should understand, being Jewish. And all that's going on."

"I'm not sure that I really do," I replied honestly.

The stories and the frightening things that were being rumored simply weren't real to me. None of the propaganda was concrete in my mind because I wasn't exposed to it. Not until later and things became much worse did the talk become reality, shattering my insulated world. It would occur five years downstream, on a very dark November night in 1938, that I would see the atrocities for myself. But for Max it was different. He was regularly exposed to the indoctrination of his parents and other German friends.

"Well, trust me, bad things are happening."

"They don't seem *that* bad to me, Max."

With his hand on my shoulder, he smiled. "Always the optimist."

A chill moved into the air. I shivered. "Time to head home."

We walked the rest of the way home in silence.

* * *

That night while unable to sleep I overheard my parents talking. I was not aware my father lost his job with the government and was stunned when I heard my mother say, "What will we do when we run out of money, Irving?"

"There is enough for now."

"And after?" Momma asked.

"I can do contracts for Jewish businesses and handle their affairs," he said.

"All your life, you worked for the government all your life. And this! This is how they pay you!"

"Shush, Rose, speak softly. The children will hear us."

My mother's raspy voice cracked. "Is it really that bad with this Hitler? Should we think of leaving?"

"This is our home. We will make do."

Leaving! I couldn't believe my ears. My parents loved Germany. My father was a successful attorney, of whom I was proud, and it seemed as if my mother was everyone's friend. She greeted every charity that graced our doorstep. Fear gripped me, and I recalled what Max said; *we're both in danger.* A rushing sensation coursed through my body, my heart was pounding, and I felt dizzy. *Get a hold of yourself,* I thought. I eventually talked myself into believing that this was all being blown way out of proportion. *Everything is fine. We'll be all right.*

As the days and weeks passed, Max's disposition worsened. I couldn't lift him from his morose mood. He had mentioned to me that his father thought we were spending too much time together and that Max needed a vacation. I hadn't understood that his father, although not a Nazi sympathizer, was deeply aware of the changes in the climate in Germany and was trying to protect Max by distancing him from Jews.

"We have a farm outside of Berlin, near Brandenburg," Max told me.

"But that's over an hour by train." I pursed my displeased lips and kicked a mound of dirt.

"I know. Ludwig," using his father's first name, "thinks the fresh air will do me some good. Oh great, I can watch the grass grow on the farmland." He sarcastically rolled his eyes and continued. "And romp in the hectares of wetland, and play by myself. I'll die of boredom."

"Sounds nice to me. I'd love to get away from all the commotion and be with you where it is peaceful around some agriculture."

"Then come with," he joked.

"Very funny. Your father would love that."

Before they left to vacation in the countryside, Max came to say goodbye. "It's a great hideaway. No longer used for farming and only occasionally for hunting." He smiled. "If my father ever falls off the edge and joins the Party, we can run away together and hide there."

While he was gone, I missed him. And I wondered if he would tell his parents about his preference if they insisted he not be friends with me. With the political weather dramatically changing, I highly doubted it.

My uneasy feelings about Max's situation and the role I played in it were nothing compared to the reality we were both about to face.

The Seven Year Dress

Chapter Three

When people I was taught to respect were openly repeating rhetoric about Aryan superiority, I had questions. How does body type or one's coloring make such a difference in the quality of their personality? I didn't understand what all the fuss was about and was sickened when I overheard a conversation between two teachers in my school. In the hallway on my way from class to recess, I passed an open door and heard something about Hitler. Curious, I leaned against a wall, pretending to fix my shoe, and listened.

"Hitler bases the Aryan race he is promoting on the premise of targeting humans for destruction who are mainly living in state-operated facilities and some private ones. Prisoners and degenerates like the feebleminded, epileptic, and homosexuals," said one of the teachers. "He wants to return humankind to Nordic roots, eliminating any taint from darker skinned races."

"And this is his idea of purging the hereditary chain?" asked the other. "He includes Jewish people in those categories. That's crazy."

"Shush, that sarcasm will get you in trouble."

Jewish people, homosexuals! Max. A wave of grief washed over me, and I choked back tears. Footsteps approached the door. I instantly stood and left.

Needing to understand more about what was happening in my country, I went to the library. Page after page of glancing through newspapers and magazine articles, my eyes took in what I believed was nonsense. Vile drivel. *The Aryan race is the master race!* This smacked in the face of my belief that Jews were the chosen people. God favored us. Reading a brief synopsis of *Mein Kampf* in a journal, I was angered. What gave this Hitler the right to decide who was good and who was bad? What makes people with light-colored hair, light-colored eyes, fair skin, and tall superior to me, to my family, to people with dark curly hair, hooknoses, dark eyes, and full lips? I moved a hand through my dense, wavy hair, feeling the thick texture as I curled the light brown strands around my fingers. I remembered my mother combing my hair and saying how lovely it was. I liked how I looked and protested to myself that my features didn't fit the descriptions I'd read about in those degrading magazines. I didn't have a hooked nose; mine was straight and small.

And so what if my eyes were brown? They were big and round and expressively beautiful, like a lot of the Germans I knew. *Blue eyes make you superior. What rubbish!* My family all had handsome features, and I was proud of their good looks.

I thought of Max, who fit the Aryan description perfectly. On the eve of his fourteenth birthday, he was handsome with his blond hair, blue eyes, and chiseled nose. His muscular frame was filling out, and he had grown to a little more than six feet, which towered over my five feet two inches.

At home that night, I looked at myself in the mirror, and again I thought of Max. *Those teachers were talking rubbish and the things I read at the library were insane.* I was raised to love myself, my family, and everyone around me. I was a confident girl. Maybe I was naïve, but I didn't think about my appearance or my religion as the most important features of who I was as a person. *Judge me on what's in my heart or my mind, not on how I look or what religion I was born into!* I discarded the garbage I had learned that day to a locked mental box: the place inside my mind where I hid things I didn't want to face or believe, what I refused to accept as real.

* * *

When Max arrived back from vacation, we met at a secluded park to catch up. He was different, more reserved. It pained me that he took his time to give me a hug. And I could have spat blood when he told me he was going to join the Hitler Youth movement on his upcoming fourteenth birthday. By then, I had read and heard enough to know this could end our friendship. Gritting my teeth, I looked around to be sure no one could hear, and asked, "Did your father convince you to do this?"

"No, it's my idea." His eyes warmed and his shoulders relaxed.

The change from his aloof composure when we greeted each other confused me. "Why?" I searched his eyes and saw in the depth of his wide pupils what I felt was resolution. A pang of tension twisted my gut.

He leaned in closer and whispered in my ear. "My father had me read Hitler's writing, and we talked about it. He believes we're either with them or against them, and being against them is dangerous."

My jaw dropped.

"Helen, it's not what you think."

"You have no idea what I think! It will be the end of us." My stomach was a tight knot.

"It will be the end of us," he breathed warm air into my ear sending a chill down my spine, and continued, "if I do nothing. You know how I feel about you. I don't care that you're a Jew. But what do you think is going to happen to you and your family? Hitler is talking about killing Jews!"

"It's just talk, Max. Try as he might, he can't hurt us with just words. What does this have to do with you joining them?" No longer able to stop myself from crying, I blurted out, "How could you?"

"I'm not joining them," he smiled, "I'm going to pretend…"

His words calmed me, easing the clumps of spasms in my neck muscles. "Huh?"

Max went on to explain that he felt the best way to protect himself was to join the Hitler Youth movement and go along with the party line. And pretend to like girls. He also saw a way to help me.

"Me? I don't see how I figure into your scheme. That's some plan, Max." I pulled back from him.

"Listen to me," he moved closer. "If something happens—"

"What?" I snapped. "What could happen?"

"Never mind all that." He took in a deep breath. "Just trust me."

What choice did I have? He was determined to go through with his stupid plan. He even swore me to secrecy. But I had to ask and had to know, "What about intimacy? Don't you ever want to know love? I mean…, you know?" I couldn't find words that weren't embarrassing.

"Of course, I do. But how would that be possible as long as haters remain in power?"

"Oh, Max." My breath caught in my throat. "What are we going to do?"

"We are going to stay alive." He grabbed my hand. "Right now, there's nothing more important than that."

Sounding wiser than his age, I couldn't argue with him. A slight breeze picked up, scattering leaves. Since we weren't sure if the noises we heard were people approaching, we took our leave of each other.

* * *

As time progressed, my parents agreed with Ludwig Müller's dictate to separate us and to break up our friendship. Once my parents discovered that Max was planning on joining the Hitler Youth, the tension between our families escalated. My parents told me I could not associate with him. Defying both our parents' orders, Max invited me to his fourteenth birthday party. I accepted. Max fought his battle with his parents, and I fought mine with my parents. I don't know which one was more difficult. With the coercion of my other siblings, especially Ben, my father finally yielded. "Just this one time, then you have to stop seeing him," he commanded.

The small victory wasn't enough for me. "He's my best friend. I won't stop being his friend!"

My mother took hold of my father's arm. "Irving, they are just children. It is not serious…"

He jerked his arm from my mother's grasp. "Children! He's joining a despicable hate group designed to become the army that will dispose of Jews!"

"Irving, not in front of the children." She hushed her tone and shooed me away with her hand. In the hallway outside of the dining room, I overheard the rest of the conversation. "What harm could come from their friendship? They have known each other all their lives. How will driving a wedge between them help any of us? Certainly Helen would be devastated. Look how she is acting out now. Her grades are already slipping." She was referring to the changes in my marks since Max told me about his plans.

My father responded. "Rose, I will not hear of my daughter being friends with a boy who is in a group that prepares its members to join the *Sturmabteilung*, the adult military wing of the Nazi Party." He coughed, loudly cleared his throat, and continued. "That wicked Hitler is disbanding all other youth organizations to ensure his power. What next from that maniac?"

Later that night, my mother came to find me. Shana was asleep in the room we shared as my mother tapped me on the shoulder. "Are you awake?"

"Yes, Mamma."

"Your father loves you, Helen. What he is doing is for your own good."

Tears escaped from my eyes. "I won't abandon my friend, Mamma. You taught me about loyalty and being a good person. I won't do it. We aren't hurting anyone," I whispered.

"I know my sweetie, but these are the times we live in." She shook her bowed head.

"You have to help me," I begged. And, eventually, my mother did turn a cheek when she knew I was sneaking out to see Max.

* * *

I received icy stares and cold shoulders from the Aryan-appearing boys Max invited to his party. He included them to keep up appearances.

One of them asked Max, "Is she a Jew?"

Max laughed as he responded, "She's just a neighbor. So what?"

So what? Brokenhearted, I left before having cake.

Much later that night, when our families were asleep, he came to find me. Pebbles bouncing off my window brought my attention to Max below, motioning for me to come outside. Max knew I was forlorn from the way I trudged toward him. My sad shoulders sagged from the weight of a mountain of dejection. "How could you not defend me?"

"Oh, Helen. I'm so sorry. That must have been awful for you. Please try to understand, I have to play these kinds of games so those *dummköpfe* believe I'm one of them," he repeated and repeated to my thickheaded, naïve protests until I broke down and cried, confident of Max's continued love and loyalty to me, but confused about why my world had become so complicated.

Max continued his charade, pretending to be everything he wasn't while convincing me he was, nonetheless, my friend. A big part of me wanted to believe he was still "My Max," but a small part of me couldn't help but wonder what kind a stranger he was becoming. Before long, the real Max would reveal himself to me.

Chapter Four

In 1933, Max and I turned fourteen. While he spent time in the Hitler Youth movement marching at rifle practice and attending the weekly meetings in his swastika-emblazoned uniform, I continued with school. My crush on Isaac Blau had evolved into a closer friendship with him. He took Max's place walking me home when classes were over. Soon we spent time strolling through parks on the weekend. I was smitten.

At the same time that I was swooning over Isaac, the German Reichstag granted Hitler dictatorial status. Shortly after the German Republic gave him this power, Jewish students were barred from attending school in Germany. That was a bleak time for Isaac and me.

One day while out on a walk with him, I knew something was terribly wrong. He walked slowly, hesitantly, as if he was balancing a stack of dishes on his head. Isaac finally stopped, looked at me and said, "We're moving away."

My heart sank. "What do you mean by away? To Leipzig? To Dresden?"

"No, much further."

"There are trains to Nuremberg. Even cross-country to Bonn. Surely, we could visit each other by train."

"I'm afraid not, Helen. We're moving to America." He lowered his head.

Stunned, I waited for him to look at me. When he did, I thought I saw what he was trying to hide. I was sure it was the sorrow he must be feeling over not just the loss of me as his girlfriend but also the loss of his homeland, the only place he'd ever lived or known. My bright-eyed Isaac was gone. In his place was a dispirited friend saying a sad goodbye.

That night my tears wouldn't allow sleep. He had told me that his parents were extremely upset when their home was robbed and defaced. Vandals had written on the inside walls of their house *Jews get out or die!* And so they were doing just that before things got worse.

My mother had a similar reaction the next morning when I told her at the breakfast table what had happened. She instantly responded that we should consider changing locations as well. But my father refused to be intimidated by this new army moving in, that they surely wouldn't displace us. He didn't want to believe the gross corruption would cost us our lives. "They are using typical bully scare tactics to harass us," he complained to my mother. "They won't kill us. Be patient and goodness will prevail." Later, his optimism would prove to be our family's ruination.

"Where shall our children go to school, Irving?" my mother asked.

"You can teach them at home."

"At home!" Momma never shouted, but her reaction came as close to yelling at Papa as I ever remembered. "Helen, Ben, Shana, and Larry all have different subjects. I have no books. Everything from their classes remains in their lockers in school. They weren't even allowed to bring them home."

My father sternly repeated, "You will teach them. You will find a way."

"What is happening, Irving?" My typically calm mother raised her voice even higher. "What is going to happen to us if we stay here?" Her eyes bore into his as if waiting for him to suggest moving.

"You listen to me." He pounded a fork on the table. "Nothing is happening we cannot handle. We will live through this inconvenience until it passes."

This inconvenience! I had lost my boyfriend and my best friend to *THIS INCONVENIENCE!* I felt like taking that fork out of my father's hand and stabbing it into the table. I wanted to scream that this was more than an inconvenience. Moving my untouched dinner away from me, I kept quiet.

My father looked to Larry. "You are the eldest. I want you to outline what you remember of your lessons for Helen's, Shana's, and Ben's grade levels. Help your mother teach them as best as you can. Look through your room for any notes, books, anything that is instructional. I will see if I can get some books to help you out." He glanced at my dish. "Helen, eat your food. You must stay healthy."

* * *

Months had passed when, at the end of 1933, a letter finally arrived from Isaac. He was living in New York with his mother's sister's family. The letter described life in the

Unites States, and he spoke about meeting other refugees from Nazi Germany. "One man, in particular, is fascinating. Mr. Albert Einstein. My parents enjoy spending time with him, indulging in what they say is the end of something called Prohibition. I overheard them talking about it being odd that the Constitution of the United States repealed this Prohibition. What does this all mean? It means they can legally drink alcohol. Can you imagine all the fuss over a drink when over there you're worried about your lives?" He rambled on as if starved for a friend to talk to. I read his words, wishing he were speaking them to me so that I could feel his warm breath on my neck. Oh, how I missed our sweet, intimate moments! I wondered if he had changed now that he was in America, free from the oppressive cloud of fear under which we German Jews lived. He wrote of things making national news, like a bridge being built in the city of San Francisco, while we were reading about the opening of a concentration camp in Dachau.

I felt the texture of the paper and ink, smelled the aroma of what I knew was Isaac's cologne, and my wistful heart was reminded of the times I spent with him. Ah, our first kiss. We never went further than our lips softly touching, just a few times and only briefly at that. But his kisses awakened a longing in my body that could not be quelled. I wanted to be touched where my mother told me only my husband could venture. My breasts had formed, and puberty found my private parts. Experimenting with my sensuality—my hands roaming and fondling my body, exploring new sensations—distracted me from my frustration and agitation. Being under the same roof with my family for days on end was getting on all our nerves. Fantasizing about Isaac's hands moving along my body helped pass the time. I looked at my hands holding his letter. He had held this letter. Oh, how I wished those same hands could hold me and satisfy the lusty hunger my young woman's body was craving.

The front door slammed, and my father screamed something, interrupting my daydreaming.

I ran to see what the commotion was about. My father appeared panting and red-faced. "Helen, get in the dining room!" Then he yelled to my mother. "Rose, get the children. Now!"

Once there, my pale, frightened mother asked, "What is it, Irving?"

He put his index finger to his lips, a signal for us to be quiet. "Shush." He shut the curtains.

Loud bangs in quick repetition rang out, followed by shrieking in the street.

"Dirty Jews!"

"Filthy pigs! You are ruining our country!"

More screaming. More loud explosive sounds like automobiles backfiring in rapid succession.

"Get down," my father commanded as loud popping noises came from outside of our home.

"Papa, what is that?" I went to him.

"Bullets, Helen. Now stay down."

Acid rose in my throat. Now I knew what it felt like to be scared to be Jewish—to be the target of hatred. Each *bang!* jolted me. I felt grateful that walls separated us from the noise and danger. That small sense of comfort lasted until my mother looked to the ceiling and whispered, "God, please God, keep us safe." Did she think they would break in and kill us? For what? We never hurt anybody. I would spend the rest of my life asking that same question: *why?*

Time passed in slow motion until the noise stopped. Shana was hysterical in Lawrence's arms, and Ben huddled in a pool of his urine next to me. My ashen-faced mother, frozen to the same spot for nearly an hour, gathered us children close to her. "It is over. We are safe."

My father, who had been crouching on the floor, finally stood. "No, we are not safe." His characteristic optimism fading, he motioned for us to sit with him at the table. "We have to learn to be careful. Do not open the door if a stranger knocks. Go out in pairs and, if accosted by anyone, ignore it. Do not defend yourself. If you come across a man in uniform and he asks a question, answer politely. Be respectful."

Squinting my eyes, I cocked my head and sighed. "Why do we have to cower to everyone? We've done nothing wrong."

"Helen, you listen to me, young lady. I will not tell you this a second time. No sass!"

"But father…"

"Irving," my mother stroked his back, "she is a child. Be gentle. They are frightened."

My father took a deep breath. He looked different to me—defeated. When he spoke, he seemed to be speaking to his shoes, not to us. His voice, always soft, was now somehow heavier. Harder. "We have to be very careful. There is more, yes. But I do not want to tell you. We have enough bad thoughts in our heads. We do not need uglier pictures in our minds and hearts."

"I want to know! My whole life's been uprooted and I have a right to know, Father," I protested.

Lawrence pounded the table in disgust. "You're not the only one in the family, Helen! When are you going to grow up? Listen to Papa!"

Shana started crying and Ben, trousers still wet, sat quietly shaking his head.

"Children," my mother's voice was soothing and gentle, "try to calm down. Take a breath." Then with a hand on top of my father's, she said, "Irving, it is time to tell our children. They need to know."

My father conceded. He told us what was happening to political resisters and to Jews throughout Germany. "In the south, there is a place, an abandoned munitions factory, near Dachau, where prisoners are being held."

"So what's wrong with that?" asked Ben. "Our prisons are overflowing and—"

"Ben," my father contracted his brows into a half-frowning concentration and continued with, "everything is wrong with that. It is not really for prisoners who committed real crimes. The prison is for people who are voicing disagreements with Hitler and his regime. An evil man named Heinrich Himmler opened a warehouse for men where they will be used as forced labor. There is talk that this…this enslavement camp will house…Jews."

"What do you mean *house Jews*?" asked Lawrence.

"Just that. The rumor is that Hitler wants Jews separated from mainstream society and put in places away from civilization."

"Why?" I asked.

"It is hard to explain this in a way you will understand. Suffice it to say Hitler is a hateful man who despises Jews. He holds false beliefs that have misplaced blame on Jews for Germany's economic problems among other things. He writes of wanting the world rid of Jewish people." My father shrugged his shoulders. "There is talk he is unstable. Who knows what he is capable of doing?"

"Why can't we form groups to protest with guns?" Lawrence looked at each of us before adding, "There must be enough Jews in Germany to band together."

"Resistance movements are forming. Meetings occur. But you must never discuss any of this or…" I watched my mother hold her breath as my father finally said, "As long as we mind our business and don't bring attention to ourselves, Hitler's soldiers and others instigating the trouble should leave us alone."

"This is really happening?" I asked. "It's not just a bunch of crazy rumors? I can't believe it."

"It is true." My mother finally exhaled. "Children, you listen to and trust your father. And we need to pray to God that things change."

In unison, we all nodded our agreement.

My mother smiled at Ben. "Go change your pants, son."

Watching Ben leave the room with his wet bottom, we broke into giggles. Although most likely a nervous response, the sound of our laughter calmed me. Even then I knew there would not be many days of laughter—or tranquility—ahead.

The Seven Year Dress

Chapter Five

As 1933 moved through 1934 and into 1935, the development of the Volkswagen Beetle prototypes centered on Hitler's explicit requirements for the "people's car." I wondered, *who are the people he is building these cars for?* My father was outraged by the news.

"To this idiot, cars are more important than human beings." His face was red as he spoke clutching his chest. He had been complaining of a sour stomach of late, and I worried when he would grab for his heart. When he saw my trembling chin, he smiled, waved his hand and said, "Ah, it is just my stomach." Although my mother's worry lingered, the rest of us watched it pass and didn't make a big fuss about it. After all, he was only forty-five.

The automobile wasn't the only headline in the news that aggravated my father. Papa told us that while Hitler continued to maintain a bearing of authority, he had designs on transforming Germany into a police state, beginning with the rearmament of its military, which went against the

1919 Treaty of Versailles. "While undergoing his covert internal operations, Hitler presents an international front as a diplomat by deftly negotiating with other European countries, expressing his desire for peace. He is a two-faced moron," my father protested.

* * *

I loved our home in West Berlin and thought we lived very well. Located off the Kurfürstendamm Strasse, near the Bahnhof Zoo train station, it was close to museums and the Philharmonic Hall. Our large two-story house was in a mixed neighborhood of successful Jewish businessmen, doctors, and lawyers and well-off German Christians. Max's parents inherited their home, which was next-door to ours, from Ludwig's father, a wealthy factory owner. My father purchased ours while being employed by the government.

Upstairs, Shana and I shared a bedroom, while Larry, Ben, and my parents had their own bedrooms. Downstairs was a formal living room, a dining room with a large table that sat ten, and an adjacent bathroom. The front door opened to a foyer with walls adorned with classic art pieces. To the right was my father's lushly furnished office where he did his paperwork. Antique vases and lamps adorned 18th-century end tables and upon his desk was a statue by Christophe-Gabriel Allegrain, the brother-in-law of the famous Jean-Baptiste Pigalle. My father prided himself on his art collection, which he claimed was a wise investment. Priceless to him, he would lose it all before too long.

After my father had been dismissed from his government job, he managed to make ends meet by doing some legal and accounting work for Jewish proprietors. When not paid with money, he accepted food and objects we could use. I remember the day he came home with a sewing machine.

"You can teach the girls to sew," he told my mother, who gave up sewing years earlier when her machine broke. "It will give them something to occupy their minds."

My mother's eyes lit up. "And perhaps we could supplement your income with tailoring for some friends?"

"A very good idea, Rose." My father nodded in approval. "Thank you, dear."

The dining room was transformed into a sewing room with thread strewn about and rags for fabric to teach us how to use the machine. While Shana and I busied ourselves learning and practicing, my father found work for us to do. Entering the room with a handful of clothes, he commented, "This should keep you busy. And an advance payment for your work." He extended a handful of Reichsmarks to my mother.

"We will go to the grocery store and buy something nice for a meal?" She smiled. "Perhaps even splurge and get chocolate for the children." Since our funds were diminishing, that would be an extravagant expenditure.

Word got around that we delivered well-sewn garments, transforming old, tattered clothing into respectable outfits. I found the work enjoyable and meaningful, and I took great pride in my newfound talent as a seamstress. Shana didn't take to it like I did.

* * *

Max was becoming a distant friend, and he would rarely sneak over to see me anymore. Through my sewing room window, I'd watch him in his uniform, marching in the street with his youth group. I wondered if his stern, blank expression held back the fear he shared with me concerning his affinity for boys. Although I missed spending time with him, there was something very comforting about knowing I had a friend who was moving up in the ranks of the Hitler Youth. That feeling helped me when, in 1935, Hitler announced the Nuremberg Laws that stripped Jewish people of their civil rights as German citizens. The new laws meant that I would be excluded from Reich citizenship because of my religion. The Nuremberg Laws also prohibited Jews from marrying or having sex with someone of German blood.

"What does this mean?" My mother asked my father about the rumored laws.

Wiping the sweat from his forehead, my father responded, "I am not sure."

"You are a lawyer! Have you read these laws?" My mother was unusually adamant that Papa explain the situation to her—and to us.

"I have seen some of the information…"

"What do you mean by information?" she asked, looking at the rest of us piling around them in the kitchen.

"Stolen papers, handwritten copies, scraps of sentences. One cannot piece it all together from limited access to the original documents."

"What did you see?" Lawrence, my oldest brother, looked so grown-up—so intense.

My mother stared at Lawrence, nodded, and then turned to my father. "Tell him, Irving. Tell us all whatever you have seen."

Shaking his head, my father took a slow, labored breath. "Rose, please…"

"Please tell us," I joined in. "We've been through this before with holding back information. You said you'd share with us. Papa, please."

"Sit," he commanded and waited for us to comply, then went on to say, "there are many laws. Over a hundred. A Jew is defined," he coughed, cleared his throat, and continued, "as anyone who has three or four Jewish grandparents. It does not matter if the person practices the religion or not. Hitler is referring to bloodline. There are a lot of Germans who have not practiced Judaism in years and do not consider themselves believers of the faith. That does not matter. Our blood is what matters to that madman and his growing gang of thugs."

"Why would someone not want to be a Jew if that was their lineage?" asked Ben.

"Ben, my boy, not everyone shares our same beliefs. Some Jews have even converted to Christianity in order to—"

"What?" I interrupted. "That can't be!"

"Yes, it is true. They are not bad people. And we are not better or right for our beliefs. People are just different. You and your friend Max had no problems because of religious differences. It is like that, Helen."

"But now Max can't come around," I moaned.

"We are not going to get into that again, Helen."

"What else should we know about the new laws?" asked Lawrence.

My father continued to explain that the new laws were an attempt to label and single out Jews. He didn't feel this would escalate into anything more serious. Once again, he believed that as long as we didn't cause trouble they'd leave us alone.

I had so many questions after what my father had told us about these new laws. How could being a Jew make me a target? A target for what? What kind of trouble was I supposed to avoid so I would be safe? I hoped that Max, being in the center of the organization creating all these new rules, might have some answers for me. Arranging a time and place to talk with him would be tricky, but I had to try. I wondered if this was the kind of thing that my father warned us against doing.

Max and I hugged for a long time. We agreed that neither of us liked to lie to our families and sneak around, but we had to do what was necessary to see each other and protect each other. He filled me in on the new laws from his perspective, including news of escalating violence in the streets. Hitler's men and those who agreed with the Nazi propaganda harassed customers of Jewish stores. Jewish sympathizers were warned not to buy things from Jews. "The laws are designed to start and implement the process of segregation, isolation, and, from what I'm hearing, much worse."

"Like what?" I couldn't imagine a worse situation.

"More violence. But what's the point of speculating right now? Just be careful, Helen."

Although I had not witnessed any of these events, I believed what Max told me was true.

Sleep eluded me most of that night. I realized that every answer I received only created many, even more taunting, questions swirling around in my mind. I felt dizzy and nauseated. Max had told me things my family needed to know, but I never shared anything Max had confided in me with my family. I had to protect him and our precious friendship. But didn't I have a duty to protect my family? Maybe I was protecting my family by shielding them from terrible truths that could damage my father's health?

A young girl shouldn't have such heavy burdens to bear.

The Seven Year Dress

Chapter Six

Just as my time with Max dwindled, so did my letters from Isaac. The last time I heard from him was in 1936 when he wrote to me about a man named Jesse Owens, an American track-and-field athlete who would be visiting Germany. Our country was hosting the Summer Olympic Games in Berlin. With the world watching so closely, Hitler didn't want the Games being transferred to another country because of international criticism of his new regime of hatred. He wanted to create the impression that all Germans were prospering, and that any news of unrest was hyped-up rhetoric. Although Jewish athletes were not allowed to participate in the Games, open hostility against the Jews quieted. The Nazi regime moderated its attacks, including taking down "Jews not welcomed" signs from public places.

With this easing of overt antagonism against the Jews, my father relented about my excommunication from Max. At least I had my best friend back and felt safe to be with him without sneaking around my parents. Max's parents were a different story. They continued to pressure him to stay away from Jews, and so he took caution when meeting me.

During dusk, we spent our time together. The darkness brought safety from what was visible; fear was still a persistent intruder each time we met. As twilight approached, we sat in my backyard watching the last of the soft glow disappear from the horizon.

"Your father has had a change of mind." Max smiled.

"He has a good heart, Max," I replied. A cold shiver moved through my body thinking about my father's health. The burden of Hitler's new Germany weighed heavily on him. Although he denied feeling ill, his pale skin told me differently. Knowing he refused to see a doctor, we tried our best to keep his spirits up. I was grateful he eased up on my relationship with Max. I didn't want him to discover that we had been stealing about to see each other and that my mother knew. "He doesn't want to see me hurt or without friends. After we got kicked out of school, I—"

"I felt horrible about that," Max interrupted.

Nodding to acknowledge what he just said, I continued. "After that," I reflected back on the guns going off in front of our house a while ago, "I was terrified by a riot in our street. Momma, Papa, all of us were scared." I told him about it. "It changed my father." Since Max joined the Hitler Youth movement, I hadn't been able to talk about the chaotic events and feelings I'd experienced. Most of our sneaking around to see each other was for me to find out about the new laws, or information he had, but we discussed very little concerning my mounting dread. Until now. "So much has changed for us Jews, Max." He nodded and listened while I shared my most personal thoughts and fears with him.

"Oh no! Gunshots in front of your home! I must have been away at that time. My parents said nothing about it to me."

"Maybe they weren't home either?"

Max smacked his lips. "I hate what's happening." His melancholy voice cracked. "And I wish we didn't have to hide our friendship."

Max talked slowly and in deeper tones than I remember. I suppose I did, too. Sorrow, fear, regret. That was the language we spoke now. "Me too. How long do you think it will continue like this?" I searched his eyes for the answer I hoped to hear. "I mean things seem to be improving a little, aren't they?"

"I'm not so sure about that," he frowned.

The ease between us moments before vanished and tension seized my chest. "What do you mean?"

"We've been told…" Correcting what he just said, "no, ordered, to ensure the Olympic Games proceed without incident."

"Without incident? What does that mean?"

Max shifted away from me, averting his eyes. "No public efforts to control the 'undesirable elements' of society."

I sighed. "So you think all the recent changes are just for show?"

"I'm afraid so," he responded, looking back at me.

"Maybe you're wrong, Max."

"I don't think I am. But," his speech became taut, and his left shoulder twitched, "we'll know for sure when the Olympics are over."

There was something about his demeanor—the unspoken caution in the way he spoke—that frightened me. I wanted something from him that was both hopeful and tangible. I wanted a sign that things might get better, or that they wouldn't get worse. *How much worse could they possibly get?* Feeling he was holding back, and knowing I wouldn't rest until I found out, I pressed him for more information.

"Why bring up things we can't change, things that will only haunt you?" he asked.

I nodded. He sounded like my father, not like my sixteen-year-old friend. He looked and acted older than I remembered. I noticed faint wrinkles on his forehead and a dullness in his eyes. Where were Max's dancing, bright eyes? What had aged him so much? "You may not understand this, but I have to know, Max. I just have to."

"You want to hear about murder?" When his voice became gravelly, he cleared his throat. "Senseless acts of violence?"

As the night grew darker and stars lit the sky, I kept quiet and waited.

Wiping his blond hair back off his forehead, he began with, "Gretel Bergmann was kicked off the team of high jumpers. Everyone in Germany knows that she is one of the world's most accomplished athletes in track and field. I heard an unconfirmed rumor that, when a few of her friends protested the injustice, they were shot. Some were wounded. Two were killed." With a finality in his words, Max added, "I suspect it is true."

"Oh no!" I jolted erect. "I can't believe it. After all she had gone through," referring to the fact that, after the Nazis had risen to power, she was prohibited from her sport for being Jewish. Her parents sent her to Great Britain where she partook in and won the British championship.

"Then Hitler wanted her returned, to put up a front as a liberal, tolerant country," said Max. "But she was not allowed to participate in the Games."

"I don't understand," I said.

"It's what I was trying to tell you about this recent change being for show."

"And people died trying to help her?" My chest felt like a ton of rocks was pressing in on it.

"That's not all. People are dying for doing nothing. You wanted to know? What I just told you is nothing compared to—"

"Nothing? How could you call people dying 'nothing'!" Releasing the frustration from feeling powerless, I slammed my fist on the bench. "It's madness!"

"How can I say that? People are being killed because of how they look. Jews are being treated worse than animals."

"Oh my God."

"You wanted to know. There it is. I'm sick about it." He put his face in his hands. "But there is nothing you or I can do about it."

Although I didn't want to accept it, I knew he was right. I knew because Max had told me that the German army under Hitler had grown to millions, with Heinrich Himmler enlisting and training hundreds for the Schutzstaffel (SS). The latter petrified me because I had heard it was established by Himmler to get rid of the "sub-humans."

The sound of gunshot in the distance and a steely look from Max over in the direction where it came from snapped me out of denial. As Max's words ricocheted in my brain, their meaning shook me to the core.

Suddenly I felt that I was the sub-human Himmler spoke about. What was left of my naivety abruptly disappeared. I was now a vermin Jew to be purged from Hitler's pristine Germany. Helen—a free, kind, loving young woman—no longer existed in the eyes of my country.

Chapter Seven

Max was right. The Olympics ended, and the hostility toward Jews returned with a vengeance. It didn't hit Berlin with full force until November 1938. Before that point, the reign of terror was frightful, but horrific devastation on a mass scale began when the world, once again, wasn't watching closely. There were singular incidents of violence, vandalism, and disruptions of Jewish businesses, but our family continued on in relative safety.

The laws that the Nazis initially put into place were not as stringently obeyed as they were in the late 1930s. I didn't mind, nor did I fully understand, the Nuremberg Laws (also known as, the Nuremberg Racial Purity Laws) when they were enacted, criminalizing sexual relations and marriage between Aryans and Jews. The prejudice and persecution they caused did not initially result in physical violence. Other than feeling offended that I was considered an object of segregation from Germans, I did not think that I was in bodily danger. But I was bothered that the laws stated that people with three or four Jewish grandparents "belonging to the Jewish race and community were not approved to have Reich citizenship." Stripped of my citizenship, my official status along with thousands of other Jews became "subjects of the state." Most troubling, though, was that Jews had no authority to influence politics, education, or industry without voting rights or representation in professional jobs.

The escalation of hostilities against Jews began with Himmler's increased power as leader of the SS, with membership climbing to over fifty thousand members strong. Under his direction, through orders from Hitler, conditions for Jews took a turn for the worse. My father told me that, although not trusted by the paramilitary Sturmabteilung (SA), the SA supported the SS and Himmler. This gave Hitler the power to control the government and political attitudes toward the Jews. Whenever my father spoke about Himmler, the hairs on the back of my neck stood on end; it was an ominous feeling. I wondered what it portended.

Being a lawyer and having a great respect for the law, my father hated the laws that were enacted to separate Jews from Aryans. He especially loathed that Aryan doctors were forbidden from treating Jewish patients, hindering their medical treatment. When I protested to Max about what I'd overheard my father say, Max told me, "What's happening is horrible, but never lose sight of the fact that opposition of any sort, or plots to overthrow the Nazis, are met with executions."

Executions! My throat seized into a lump that made it hard to swallow. It was difficult to refrain from sharing these conversations with my family. But I assumed that my father had already heard these things by the way he looked lately. I learned a few days later I was right not to say anything to him. My father had just returned home from collecting clothing for me to mend when I heard my mother ask him, "Are you all right?"

"Yes, yes." He put down the bundle of clothes as I entered the living room. Ben was following me.

"Papa, you don't look well." I motioned for him to sit on the couch. "Put your feet up. Relax."

"I am fine." He waved a hand as if to dismiss the concern we expressed at his obvious pastiness. Remaining standing, he told us, "Today was not a good day. I need to speak with the family. Where are Lawrence and Shana?"

"Shana is upstairs, and Lawrence is out back," said my mother.

"Ben, please go get them." Papa turned to my mother. "Rose, could you please make me a cup of tea? Chamomile. Perhaps a pot? Enough for all of us."

My father only drank Chamomile tea when he was worried. Now I was nervous. What did he want to tell all of us? Thinking of the worst, I assumed he had bad news about his health. I sat down and patted the place next to me. "Papa, please come sit by me." Helping him was the only thing that mattered to me, that and not making him self-conscious. I said, "I need my Papa's warmth next to me. It's cold today."

He smiled and sat by me. "Helen, it's 73 degrees outside."

Putting my arm through his, I felt hot sweat pouring from him. Afraid to say the wrong thing, I decided to say nothing.

Lawrence came in with Ben. "You wanted to see me, Papa?" asked Lawrence.

"Where is Shana?" My father looked past my brothers.

"I told her," said Ben, his voice a few pitches higher than usual. "She should be here."

My mother went to the foot of the stairs and yelled, "Shana, come now! We are waiting for you." Moments later, Shana scuffed down the stairs. My mother narrowed her eyes and tapped her toe when she directed her displeasure at Shana. "Pick up your feet when you walk. Too many pairs of shoes are worn out that way."

"Yes, Mamma." She smacked her lips and rolled her eyes.

The pressure of living under constant fear must have had gotten to my twenty-four-year-old sister. Yes, she must sorely miss a time when she was allowed to be a carefree young woman! None of us were immune to the dread that was now part of the air we breathed, but Shana's moods had gone from irritability to petulance, which she took out on the rest of us. Her quarrelsome antics were getting on my nerves. I suppose we were all getting on each other's nerves in some way.

Noting her sarcasm, my father sat up. "That is enough, Shana! Go sit down." He slowly glanced around the room. When his eyes fell on the window, he got up and shut the curtains, folding them over each other. "Keep these closed from now on. Our business at home is private. Understood?"

When his facial pallor flushed red, Mamma told Papa, "Sit down. Please. Tell us what is happening."

He took a sip of tea and said, "There are some very bad men policing the streets. You must avoid them." He went on to tell us that Himmler's Gestapo (the Nazi secret police) was spying on Jews. They were enlisting informants, including Jewish people, to report on any resistance to Hitler's regime. The Gestapo was silencing political opponents or Jewish sympathizers. That day, my father had heard about a shop owner protesting to his customers about the injustice of the boycotts. Among the people in the store were two secret police officers. Mistaking the Gestapo for safe patrons, others snickered in agreement. The spying Gestapo drew guns and ordered the shop owner into the street, onto his knees, and shot him in the head. They then returned to the store and beat up everyone there, including innocent bystanders. "I was told that the Gestapo gunmen screamed, 'let that be a lesson,' and 'next time it will be worse for those of you who dare to sneer!' They clicked their heels, saluted 'Heil Hitler!' and left the store." My father frowned in disgust and continued. "Instigating Jews to report on Jews. It will destroy whatever trust there is in our dwindling community."

"Who was the store owner Papa?" I asked, wanting to know if we knew the man.

"Helen, who he was is not important. It could have been anyone of..." Lowering his head, he broke down in tears. Papa knew the man who was killed. Maybe we all did.

My mother spoke in the kind of whisper she used whenever I was sick or frightened, but she was talking to Papa. "Tell us, Irving. To see you this upset, he was obviously someone you were fond of. Get it off your chest."

As if the word "chest" was an omen, my father's hand flew to his chest just as his breathing became labored. He tried to say something, but all he could do was open and close his mouth like a fish on land.

My mother screamed for Lawrence to phone Dr. Schecter. "Tell him to come immediately!"

When my father started to froth at the mouth, I panicked.

"Get a washcloth, Helen!" Momma gently laid Papa's head on her lap while I stood paralyzed. "Now, Helen!" My mother's urgent voice shocked me into motion. I ran to the kitchen for a washcloth.

With my father's head on my mother's lap, we huddled around him and waited for the doctor to arrive. I cursed the amount of time it was taking and blamed that damn evil Hitler for forbidding us entry into hospitals. Since German physicians and facilities denied Jews treatment, we had to rely on Jewish doctors' houses and small offices for care.

By the time Dr. Schecter arrived, my father's breathing had become increasingly labored. "He is having a heart attack." The doctor signaled Lawrence. "Bring a blanket. We need to keep your father warm." He instructed Shana. "Bring me a glass of water." I was relieved that she obeyed him without hesitation.

Dr. Schecter gave Papa a pill. He told Mamma, "This will calm his heart and keep blood clots from forming. Keep him quiet and hydrated. No salt or stimulating foods."

"What are those?" I asked as Lawrence returned and put the blanket over papa.

"Alcohol and caffeine. Keep him downstairs. Bed rest until I can return in a week. Only up to go to the bathroom. No exertion or excitement and he should be fine."

"Are you sure? With no hospital care or…" my mother pulled at the cuffs of her sleeves.

"Yes, Rose. What I've done here is what I would have done at the hospital. Just do your part and keep him calm." Looking around the room, he said, "All of you. Do your part. His heart can't be excited."

"I do not know that he will stay calm, Dr. Schecter." My mother wrung her hands. "I'm worried that with—"

Schecter interrupted, handing my mother a box of pills. "Here is something to calm him and help him sleep. Give him one a day. That is enough to keep him sedated until I can return." By the time Dr. Schecter left, the medication was taking effect. Papa was nodding off.

We never found out who the Gestapo killed that day. We wouldn't ask and were never told. And too many similar scenes started to occur to try to figure out which one my father had referred to. I hated the Gestapo! I hated the man named Himmler! I hated Hitler! If anger had entered Papa's heart and nearly broke it, I understood; I felt its acid eating away in my chest, too. *Those bastards!* The lesson my mother had taught us about how holding on to hatred is the same as swallowing poison seemed like a child's fairy tale. I had grown up and was now facing a terrible reality—I was frightened, hurt and angry. Horrible people were torturing innocent people. I hated them and wanted to harm them. And I was clinging to my hatred for dear life.

Chapter Eight

As my father was resting and healing, my siblings and I continued to bring in some money. I carried on with my sewing jobs while Lawrence and Ben did carpentry and handyman work for people in the neighborhood. Shana helped around the house as Mamma tended to Papa.

At the same time as my father regained his health and a rosy color returned to his cheeks, I was undergoing changes as well. My sensuality was in full bloom as I approached my nineteenth birthday. Sewing and reading failed to alleviate the sexual urges building in my body, so I tried to quell persistent waves of passion by exploring my body. My large breasts were fully formed, and I found great pleasure in stimulating my nipples while I imagined kissing sweet Isaac. At night, once Shana was asleep and snoring, I gave into my primitive, carnal instincts by letting my mind and hands take me to places I never dared venture before. Satisfying my physical needs also helped me release some of the pent-up hostility that I was feeling from all the injustices and suffering surrounding me.

* * *

When my father was feeling better, he started to do more around the house, but at a slower pace. We all forbade him from working the way he did before his heart attack. "Your life is more important. And Helen has taken on extra sewing work from Max," my mother told him. He didn't protest. My mother was both relieved and amazed. "I wonder what is in those pills the doctor gave him," Momma whispered as she winked at me. I shrugged and smiled.

What I didn't tell Papa was that Max had continued his ruse by joining the SS. He had worked his way up in the ranks of the Hitler Youth movement as a leader with merits. One of the youth directors recommended him for a clerical SS position. Now having a salary, he rented an apartment and could help me. Jews were being used for cheap labor. Under the guise of working for him, I could get out of the house and spend more time with Max while earning money for my family.

He also referred me to men he worked with to do their sewing. The idea of doing anything for anyone involved in the grievous acts against Jews gave me a stomachache. But with my father no longer working the odd jobs he used to pick up, we needed the money. Learning to be of service and catering to the enemy became a valuable lesson for me; indeed, it would save me.

My mother agreed that, since Max would arrange and bring the sewing to his apartment for me to pick up, my new job was safe enough. I assumed that, even in the German police, there were most likely good men—like Max. That operating assumption helped me feel better about my work.

Little did I know then that, regardless of a man's basic decent nature, orders were to be taken seriously, especially when the stakes were raised. Ethics? Morals? To hell with them!

Max, with his secret, would prove to be a rare exception. Working for him mending clothes turned out to be fruitful. In addition to what Lawrence and Ben earned, the cash I brought in helped to make ends meet. There was even a little extra for the occasional treat; chocolate was our favorite. Our collective efforts appeared to help my father regain his health. And once Papa's positive attitude returned with outbursts of gratitude, a cappella singing found its way back into our home. Sitting in the living room, we'd hum, whistle, and sing in soft voices. When my father led us in a song, I sobbed, stopping everyone cold.

"What is it, Helen?" my mother asked.

"The words." I was referring to the lyrics about God sheltering us and keeping us strong. I didn't remember all the lines but knew it was a Hebrew song my father had taught us in our childhood. Knowing the verses wasn't important, knowing God was.

My father tilted his head to the side, smiled broadly, and placed a hand over his healing heart. "Yes, my darling, this strength cannot be taken from us. Not with words or threats. And not with guns or violence. And always remember above all else, this gift of life is the most important. It's our gift from God, to be valued always. When there is life, there is a chance and reason for hope. One never knows what the future will bring, but as long as we are alive, there is the possibility for something good. Trust in the goodness and kindness of people. And no matter what, never, never give up. Make this your sustaining attitude. This can never be taken from you."

That day was precious to me. My whole family was together, happy and hopeful. With the hymn still in the air and my father's words in my heart, I had faith that God would protect us. But would that sustain me if the future brought something more horrible? I wondered what would come and how I would feel. Before long, my conviction would be put to the test.

As if reading my mind and sensing my hesitation, my father said, "God is always with us, my child. Do not doubt Him, and He will not forsake you.

Shana, usually in her own world, asked, "What of the violence? All the harm being done to our people."

"Shana, come here, my sweetheart." My father opened his arms, beckoning to her. She went to his lap. We were never too old to sit in our Papa's lap. "There are no words to help me explain this. It is a sense, from the deepest intuitive place in my soul that understands this whole divine play of life is under His control, not ours. You need to find that place in your soul. It's there. For everyone."

Shana sat erect and raised her voice when she said, "God doesn't kill innocent people. I refuse to believe that!"

"No, He doesn't. People do that to each other."

"Why?" She covered her face with her hands.

"Shush," he whispered in her ear. "Calm yourself. Be still." Rubbing her back, he continued, "Take a deep breath and feel your body. Notice the life within you." He hugged her close to him and repeated what he had said to us earlier. "The gift of life is what is important…" He looked at her, then gazed at each of us around the room, and then continued, "We are not bestowed with the wisdom of what to do with the life we are given. That is out of our control. Men go astray, Shana, but that is not the fault of God."

"I don't believe that! I don't believe that." She burst into tears.

"Let it out." My mother went to Shana's side and gave my father a warm smile. She touched his cheek and said, "Irving, she needs to get it out of her. Let it be."

Lawrence, Ben, and I watched my sister break down and cry a wail to stir the dead. I began to cry—for myself, for my family, Max, and for all the guiltless who were subjugated by the repulsive oppression that had darkened Germany. What started with a song ended with grief. Day in and day out, this was how our lives unfolded: on an emotional roller coaster.

Several days later, as I was coming down the stairs for breakfast, I heard a loud crash in the kitchen. I rushed in just after my father. Shana, Lawrence, and Ben were still upstairs. My mother was crouched on the floor next to a shattered platter that had held eggs and pancakes. Making no attempt to clean it, she whimpered to my father, "My sister gave me that dish for our wedding."

He took a slow and deliberate breath in an attempt to move air through his constricted chest. Fearful of the cumulative effect the emotional turmoil was having on him, I went to help him with my mother. He put a hand on my mother's arm to help her up—a mere gesture of support from an ailing but loving husband. His heavy, weary eyes locked with mine. Then, with a gentle nod, he told me to leave them alone.

Without a word, I exited and stood on the outside of the door to eavesdrop. My mother's crying intensified. My father's voice soothed, "Oh my darling, Rose. I'm so sorry…"

Mamma's voice cracked. "You…you are…are sorry?"

"If I had not taken the job with the government in Berlin, we would still be living near your family in Munich." Most of our extended family lived there: my father's two brothers and my mother's entire family. We hadn't seen our uncles, aunts, and cousins in several years.

She mumbled something unintelligible, and then the room went silent. Even with one ear pressed up against the wall, I couldn't discern the rest of the conversation. This wouldn't be the last time I listened to their private conversations. A few nights later when I couldn't sleep, I paced the floor outside their room. They were talking quietly. My mother reacted to my father's plea to God for help. "Where is God now? The help has not come." She said more, but she lowered her voice, so it was inaudible.

When my father erupted with, "*Sheket Bevakashah!*" I gathered what Mamma said was not nice. I knew it was Hebrew for "quiet please.*"

My father rarely spoke Hebrew, so it surprised me to hear him say this. We didn't adhere to strict Jewish tradition and laws; my mother didn't even keep kosher. Papa understood that it was easier for her when entertaining his non-Jewish friends while employed with the government. The only religious event I recall my family observing was the Passover Seder. The rules of our religion did not define us, yet others were defining us by our religion. This pathetically sad irony labeled us for extinction.

They argued back and forth, but when my mother started sobbing loudly enough for me to hear, my father's voice softened. The conversation ended with them whispering.

Aside from spying on family conversations and indulging myself in my private, intimate explorations at night, I looked forward to visiting Max. He kept the sewing jobs coming and, as anxious as I felt, I enjoyed having a reason for being out in public.

* * *

Excited to see Max, I opened the closet I shared with Shana and thumbed through my dresses. I especially looked good in a couple of them that clung to my waist and hips. I was proud of my body, its shape with a narrow waist, flat stomach, rounded hips, but I felt self-conscious about my bountiful breasts. I attributed that to Mamma's constant admonishing me to "cover yourself up" and "your body is for your husband to see." All I knew was that, alone at night, touching them gave me pleasure.

After trying on both dresses, I decided on the floral magenta with dark pink flowers and green leaves. Looking in the mirror, I thought to myself it looked perfect. In the bathroom, I brushed my brown shoulder-length hair back off my neck into a tight bun. I didn't want my curly hair to go frizzy. After applying light rouge to my cheeks and a blush of rose to my lips, I went back to my closet and took my coat off a hanger. Putting it on and buttoning it to the neck, I knew it would lessen Mamma's concern about me being seen on the streets.

On my way out, I heard Momma and Papa laughing in the kitchen. I didn't want to know why; it was enough that they were happy. A smile came from somewhere deep inside of me and wouldn't let go. Those were the good times.

On that mild summer day, I was in a better mood than I had been in a very a long time. I made my way to the main street, three blocks from my house. Passing people on bicycles, seeing couples walking hand-in-hand, smiling to a woman pushing a baby carriage, and nodding to a man sweeping the sidewalk, I was reminded of what my life had been like before Hitler came to power. Nostalgia overwhelmed me as I continued past lush trees lining the familiar street, the eclectic stone façade architecture, and the aroma of wurst and fresh-baked bread coming from stores and cafes. I was born and raised in Germany. She was my country, and I loved her. I longed for my old friend back.

Two men in uniform approached me, interrupting my thoughts. Acid rose into my tightened throat. My neck muscles tensed. My fond and wistful musings vanished along with the serenity they gave me. The reality of Hitler's Germany hit me: I should never feel safe walking through Berlin. I prayed they didn't stop me. I prayed I didn't look Jewish. Averting my eyes, I took a relaxed breath when they passed me without a word. The image of the swastika on their arms stayed in my head as I rushed to Max's apartment with my head lowered.

Turning the corner onto Max's residential apartment lined avenue, I felt more at ease. The uniformed men were gone and, aside from a couple of children playing outside, the street was empty. I took in a deep, much-needed breath.

"You look lovely." Max greeted me by smiling and waving me into his home.

Removing my coat, I looked around his tidy, 700 square-foot apartment and noticed that he had painted the walls. "You did all this since my last visit?" I walked into the tiny living room with only enough space for a couch, desk, and chair.

"Yes," he smiled.

"When do you have time to do this?"

Laughing, he replied, "Very funny. I do get an occasional day off." He followed me as I walked past the kitchen, noticing he had cleaned the stove and hung knickknacks on the refrigerator.

Down a three-foot hallway was a bedroom with a minuscule closet, and a bathroom. "You like the color scheme?" He smiled. "If it's not a decorating trend, it should be. A different color for each room. Very modern, yes?"

"It looks great, Max. So alive!"

When we reached the bedroom, he said, "Yellow for you." He knew I loved yellow.

"Ah, that's so sweet of you. When you're in here resting, you can think of me sending kind thoughts to you. And it's a nice light touch for a bedroom. It goes well with that plaid spread," I commented on the red and dark blue geometrical design of the material.

Max puffed out his chest. "I finally get to arrange my things the way I want them." A big smile came over his face, and he lit up when he said, "My father, being ultra-conservative, wouldn't allow this degree of colorful flamboyance."

We both laughed. It felt so good to be just who we were, two friends spending time together. And having fun.

"Come, let's have some tea."

That day there was no talk of Germany, Jews, or work. We indulged only in light banter. As our time together was ending, Max confessed he had a crush on a man he worked with. "If anyone ever overhead this…" He blushed.

I made a closing-zipper motion across my lips. "Your secret is safe with me." There was a new relaxed comfort about Max, and I wondered if the hues on the walls were more than a minor rebellion against his strict father. Was it a way for him to express his repressed nature?

When it was time for me to leave, he handed me a stack of three garments that needed mending. We agreed on when I would return them. I put my coat back on, hugged him, and left.

On my way home, I thought of my visit with Max. He had found a way to express himself and be happy in this oppressive regime. It gave me hope that maybe I, too, could carve out a "normal" life for myself—one filled with a lover and future.

Chapter Nine

As summer moved into fall, I continued with my sewing duties while Lawrence and Ben scouted Jewish neighborhoods for odd jobs. Shana rediscovered her passion for baking and devising ways to be creative with limited ingredients. Her disposition improved dramatically. One of my favorites was her banana bread pudding. I loved to hear Shana's humming while making noises with the beater—clanging pots and pans were music to my ears as she filled the house with the aroma of cinnamon and vanilla. She also helped prepare meals, which gave Mamma time to spend with my father to ensure his health remained stable. Dr. Schecter urged him to take it easy through winter, which, he told us, is harder on coronary circulation. "Come spring, you'll be ready to do part-time work if you want to," he told my father.

"That is good news, doctor," said Papa. I was happy to see the encouraging smile on my father's face.

"Well, I have other patients to see."

I handed him his coat and, as he was putting it on, he lifted his head to inhale a pleasant cinnamon scent coming from the kitchen. "What might that be?" He smiled.

My mother came out with gaily-wrapped goodies that Shana had baked. "Cookies and a spice cake—a thank you for all your help. Shana is excellent in the kitchen." She handed the treats to Dr. Schecter.

"My wife will appreciate this." He accepted the package. As he turned to leave, he stopped. "You know," he said, "if you want to make a little extra money, perhaps Shana could sell her baked goods. From what I am smelling, I am quite sure some of our friends in the neighborhood would be interested." He patted my mother on the back.

With that boost to Shana's morale, she doubled her baking efforts, using leftover bread to make puddings and overripe fruit for muffins. Before long, she was helping to increase the family income.

While my family had found an acceptable way of surviving under the oppressive political regime, the Nazis were focusing on reclaiming Germany's lost territories and expanding into Czechoslovakia and Poland. The newspapers mainly wrote Hitler's propaganda, but I learned what was really occurring on the international front from Max. He told me that when Jews were displaced and relocated to ghettos, resistance movements flared up. The geographical changes in 1938 began with Hitler's intrusive crusade for Lebensraum—the territory that Hitler felt was needed for the natural development of Germany. Britain, France, and Russia, not wanting to go to war with Hitler's army, assuaged the German bully. Because of this, Germany was able to annex neighboring Austria without bloodshed and divide up Czechoslovakia. I was shocked when I heard that no countries challenged this violation of the Treaty of Versailles. The choice of appeasement instead of military confrontation enabled a shift in the climate that allowed for Hitler's pogrom, which was on the horizon.

I wished I could have shared the information Max continued to trust me with, but I had given him my word. I kept silent when I learned much more about what was happening in Germany. While geographical encroachment continued, state programs were changing as well. Initially set up as a camp to house political prisoners, Dachau concentration camp was expanded by Himmler to hold forced-labor detainees. Soon it would become the place where Jews were imprisoned. Himmler worked hand-inglove with Sigmund Rascher, the doctor who was in charge of medical experiments at Dachau. Rumors circulated that Rascher was in cahoots with Hitler's personal medical doctor, Dr. Karl Brandt, to design and carry out programs of involuntary euthanasia. Under the rationale called racial hygiene, the murder of millions of Jewish people and other undesirables would soon begin.

While political tension was building with Germany's hostile takeover of other countries, my family was uninformed about what was happening. Except for the rumors circulating in Berlin.

At Max's apartment, he told me he was getting a new position with the SS. Still clerical, he would be dealing with secret information. His security clearance would be much higher, too. "I've seen things, Helen. Sensitive things. It scares me."

"What's going on?" I nervously picked at a cuticle.

"Whatever I tell you, you mustn't tell anyone. Not even your family." He took a hard swallow. "This can't slip out."

"You don't have to keep saying that to me. I haven't said anything you've told me to anyone!" I pulled back from him. "Don't you trust me?"

He reached a hand to my shoulder and pressed firmly. "I do. I do, but this is very sensitive. I needed to say that."

I took hold of his hand and felt our sweat comingle. "I understand. Go on." It was an effort for me to breathe the toxic air that seemed to have entered the room.

He explained that security leaks were dealt with severely. "Anyone engaged or suspected of being engaged in violations will be punished or killed. You. Me. Anyone."

Finding it hard to accept and knowing Max liked to exaggerate his importance and, at times, his stories, I wasn't sure how to react to him. "You're kidding? You're blowing something you heard out of proportion, right?"

"No, Helen, not this time. I'm dead serious." Reconsidering, "Never mind." He shook his head, and then looked at me, probably deciding that saying more would be too risky.

But he had already said too much. My curiosity was piqued. I wanted to know anything that could put my family in danger. I begged him to tell me, swearing I'd keep my mouth shut. "What could be worse for you, what you've already confided to me or whatever this is?" When he didn't respond, I knew it was bad. His reticence was making me more nervous than I already was. Tightly wound, my throat dry, my voice wobbled. "You've trusted me all your life." Sitting next to him on the couch, I let go of his hand and wiped the wetness off mine on my dress. Pensive and brooding, conflict blemished his handsome face. My stomach turned sour. With certitude, I raised my voice, and once again I pleaded my case. "You know you can trust me! I need to know. I have a right to know."

Finally yielding, he began with telling me about secret plans to expand a concentration camp in Dachau—from political prisoners to others. He used the words "death camps."

"Who are the others?" I plucked a loose piece of skin I'd been picking at off my finger.

He pulled his moist shirt away from his chest and wiped his forehead with the back of his hand. "I don't know for sure. But I have a very bad feeling…"

So did I. The toxic air was spreading. I no longer needed validation for what I'd already suspected as true. Talk of outbursts in the streets with Jews being beaten to death and young girls being raped were more than rumors. Now I knew the horrible stories were not just idle, exaggerated gossip passed on to create fear and subjugation. The unimaginable propaganda was real. The dark circles under Max's young eyes and the worry lines etched too deeply on his face told me what I didn't want to accept. I was living in a nightmare from which there was no escape.

What I didn't know was how unthinkable it would become.

The Seven Year Dress

Chapter Ten

At the beginning of November 1938, the United States was still reeling from Orson Welles's broadcast of his adaption of H.G. Wells's, *War of the Worlds*. I read in the newspaper that the radio show sent the nation into a panic. Americans thought that space aliens had landed on their home soil. While America was reeling from a fictional crisis, Germany was facing a real national disaster. That ominous feeling Max and I shared in his apartment a couple of months earlier was about to flare into an unimaginable nightmare.

On the 7th of November 1938, a German-born Polish-Jewish refugee, Herschel Feibel Grynszpan, entered the German Embassy in Paris and shot the German diplomat, Ernst vom Rath. He died two days later. Hitler was livid. He dispensed his close and devoted associate—the vicious Joseph Goebbels—to handle the situation. Goebbels, known for his deep-seated, virulent anti-Semitism from an early age, started the retaliation on all Jews in Germany.

Goebbels gave a speech at a Nazi party meeting. It was in this speech that he told SS officers to use the SA to inflict violence on Jews, making sure the attacks appeared both spontaneous and instigated by the German people, not the SS. Jews were no longer safe; they were to be assaulted in the streets and synagogues. Jewish businesses throughout Germany were to be demolished. Goebbels's retaliation for the murder of one German diplomat paved the way for Hitler's pogrom, the annihilation of an entire population.

On the eve of November 9th, Max attempted to warn me of the danger all Jews faced. He telephoned with a message that he had a large sewing job he needed me to complete before morning. "Come to my place now." He spoke rapidly in a voice so hushed that I could barely make out what he said next. "My place now! It's an urgent matter."

The commanding tone in his voice, similar to Nazi orders I'd overheard in the street, startled me. "Max, what—"

"Now! It's important!" He hung up.

Just as I was getting ready to leave, the telephone rang again. Max's voice was less forceful but just as low. "Wear a warm coat and cover your head with a scarf and hat.

Walk slowly. Be careful. I don't want your illness to relapse."

"What's th—"

He cut me off with another hang-up. *My illness? What was he talking about?* Although late, I found my parents reading in the living room and told them I was going to collect work from Max. Daylight had long diffused into night, and the darkness crept through a crack in the curtains covering the window.

My father looked at the clock on the wall. "At this hour? It is too late for you to be out."

"He said it was urgent." I pleaded my case. "I don't want to lose my work with him. I will be very careful."

My mother looked at my father. "She will be fine. She knows not to attract attention."

"Papa, please!"

The moment he smiled and nodded agreement, I gave him a hug. Since his heart attack, he had been more agreeable. Perhaps the medication had affected his mood. Maybe he simply didn't have the energy to argue. Whatever the reason, he wasn't as excitable, and that had to be good for his heart. When I left, Shana was in the kitchen with Lawrence, and I assumed that Ben was upstairs.

Max's cryptic communiqué puzzled me until I was out on the street and understood that his phone might not have been safe. Not too far from our front door, I heard something strange that sounded like glass breaking. Then came popping sounds. At first, I thought it might be a celebration, but the closer I came to the main thoroughfare, and the louder it got, I knew differently. When I turned the corner to see what was happening, I nearly fell over. I witnessed men in ordinary dark suits with cans of black paint marking stores with the Star of David. Following them were others—including the ruffian brown-shirt SA— with clubs, smashing windows and vandalizing buildings. This open hostility with the destruction of Jewish property was new. New and terrifying.

Panic gripped me. My heart sped up so fast I feared I might pass out. I lowered my head and trod slowly, desperately trying not to draw attention to myself.

"Hey you!" A man with a forceful, loud voice shouted in my direction. Just as I was about to stop and turn, I heard gunshots. Then a sickened *thud*. I was sure it was a body that hit the ground. Drenched in sweat, I maneuvered my way through the commotion.

I kept moving, head down, walking slowly past people who stood to watch the carnage in stunned disbelief. Muttered words came from victims trying to hide, to find shelter, or to get away. I heard "Oh my God," and "This can't be happening," over and over as I moved through what felt like a march to my execution. When a mother carrying her infant child tripped, I wanted to stop to help her. I didn't. I kept walking with my head down, fearing for my life. Moving through this madness and getting to Max were my sole objectives.

Someone slapped the baby; it stopped crying. The mother wept. More gunshots. She, too, went quiet. Now I muttered, "Oh my God."

A man with a bone protruding from his broken arm tried to crawl away from his assailant as he was kicked to death.

The longest walk of my life took me through devastation beyond comprehension. Buildings defaced or in flames. Men forced into trucks or brutalized on the street for resisting capture. Women and children trampled over or silenced with beatings.

As I approached the corner that led to Max's residential street, I came to Mr. Fineburg's grocery store. A man was spray-painting the Star of David on the window, marking it for destruction. Mr. Fineburg asked, "Why?" His innocent and sensible question cost him his life. Two men dragged him out to the street in front of his store. They shoved him to his knees, and he was shot execution-style in the back of his head. His screaming wife and hysterical children witnessed the whole thing along with me.

The contents of my stomach rose into my mouth. I had to inhale slowly to prevent myself from vomiting my meal on the sidewalk. *Walk slowly.* By the time I left the annihilation behind me and turned onto Max's street, I was in a state of shock.

The watershed moment that would forever change the lives of millions of Jewish people arrived that night. Hitler's vengeance had escalated, and I could not imagine anything worse. Little did I know that nothing close to the worst had happened yet.

Chapter Eleven

Max opened the door. I stood frozen in shock, unable to speak. He grabbed the collar of my coat, pulling me into the foyer of his apartment. My knees gave out, and I fell to the floor. I can't imagine what he felt when he left me there to get a cold, wet washcloth. Kneeling down on the tile next to me, he dabbed the beads of sweat from my forehead.

The first word out of my mouth was. "Why." Still dazed, I moaned *why* over and over.

"You're as white as a ghost." He moved the cool cloth over my nose and cheeks.

I focused on him and then scanned his living room to bring myself back from the dark place into which I had descended. "Why, Max?" I cried. "Why?" I heard myself screaming.

"Helen, hush. If anyone hears you…" He had taken an enormous risk bringing me, a Jew, to his apartment that night. Anything out of the ordinary, any irregularity, was instantly under suspicion. The *Polizeistaat* (police state) was created to ensure that everyone did as they were instructed or suffer the consequences. And the police, controlled by Himmler's Gestapo, acted as they pleased to implement their orders. Starting with early indoctrination in the Hitler Youth movement, police and soldiers were programmed to follow orders without hesitation or question. Thankfully, Max had not been indoctrinated like the other sheep following the herd. He helped me to understand that the police could make an arrest based merely on a suspicion that a person was about to do something against the regime. Max's voice came back into focus. "Shush. Please, Helen, calm yourself."

Oblivious to what he just said, I screamed again, "No!"

Max slapped me in the face. Hard. "Snap out of it!" he hissed just above a whisper. "Your life depends on it. And so does your family's."

Hearing him mention my family sent a rush of fear flooding through my body. Still sitting on the floor, I pressed my back into the wall for support. Locked in fright and not fully comprehending the danger that my family was in, I stared at the door. Max sat beside me, both of us quiet until I told him I felt strong enough to walk. He helped me up, and we went into his living room. There he told me about what he had seen at work earlier that night—the orders passed down from one of Hitler's right-hand men, Goebbels.

I had witnessed the execution of those orders. "Why?" I wiped my face and blew my nose on a tissue until it shredded. Dangling it from my hand made Max laugh. It helped to ease the mood.

"I've more than one," he smiled. He took the soiled one from my hand, threw it out, and handed me the box of tissues. "You really want to know why?"

I looked at him through tear-stained eyes. Blinking to clear my vision, I saw his pained look. My best friend was drowning in an ocean of tired sorrow. His essence wept for me, for what he knew was happening and for what would continue to happen. I knew. I had seen those wounded eyes too many times. "Yes. Tell me." I cried from a place so deep that I scared myself. Max held me tightly until I finally stopped, too exhausted to weep. Too tired to feel.

"Helen, I will say this, and then we have to go. Time is on our side for a very short while, and then…." He looked around the living room as if making sure no one could see or hear us.

A stab of panic returned when the word *then* conjured the image of poor Mr. Fineburg. "My parents! My family!" I pulled myself away from him. "Max, are they in danger?"

Probably fearing I would start screaming again, he jumped up and whisked me into the hallway by his bedroom. He held my shaking body and breathed his answer into my ear. "Yes." His hand covered my mouth. "Don't scream." A cold chill ran through my body. All my urgent *whys* no longer mattered. We sprang into action as he explained his plan. "Sit there," he pointed to the living room couch, "while I grab a few things for you." I could hear him opening the bathroom drawers and cabinets. He came back with an overnight bag and set it next to me. He then packed kitchen items and food.

He handed me a pair of his pants and a man's coat. "Put these on over your clothes." Giving me one of his hats to wear, he said, "Tie your hair back before you put this on." Looking at me up and down, he asked, "Your shoes. What size do you wear?"

"Seven."

He went back to his room and returned with a pair of black shoes. "Try these on over yours."

Max did his best to make me look like a male friend. If he was seen with me, a Jewish woman, it could be the end for both of us. Informants were everywhere. German citizens did not hesitate to report suspicious activity, nor did Jews who were enlisted to snitch on other Jews. Fear and the will to survive motivated an epidemic of misguided obedience to detestable anti-Semitic rules. So Max made me look like a man.

We made it safely around back to his garage and closed the door shut. He had me get into the trunk of his car. Keeping my nose and mouth clear, he handed me a bottle of water, covered me with a blanket and whispered, "There's plenty of air in here. Stay calm."

On pins and needles in that stifling compartment, I sweated it out in the uncomfortable, hot trunk until the car stopped. I heard a door open, and then another. When both closed, I thought I heard someone get on the floor of the back seat. We continued at a slow speed for what felt like twenty minutes. When we stopped and the trunk opened, we were at an isolated quiet country road on the outskirts of Berlin. And to my great relief, standing next to Max was my brother Ben.

It was then Max told me that he had made arrangements with Ben via a "highly confidential communication." Ben was instructed to sneak out of the house and meet Max near a café they knew about in a quiet non-Jewish neighborhood. Ben and Max had remained close through the years even though my brother hated that Max had joined the SS. Ben knew Max was a good person, and that I trusted him. Max made the urgency of the situation very clear to my brother.

Max also told us that, earlier that night, he had seen the top-secret memo that said Jewish men were going to be transported to concentration camps. Non-compliance would not be tolerated. Max knew what that meant. He also knew that my father would not go quietly. I sat up and hugged Max for helping us. And hugged Ben for trusting our friend.

"We need to hurry now," said Max. "Ben, you need to get into the trunk with Helen. It'll be a tight fit, but you'll be fine until we get where we're going." Max looked at me. "Helen, you can tell him what I told you before we left. We need to get going!"

Tucked under the blanket, we had barely enough room to move. I explained to my brother that Max was taking us to his isolated farm on the outskirts of Brandenburg. Since there was only room for two in the trunk of his car, Max would switch the car for a truck that his family left at the farm. He would then return to Berlin with the farm truck for the rest of our family.

* * *

The temperature was a cool 32 degrees at the farm when we arrived. Ben and I were still warm from huddling together for what must have been an hour trip. My entire body ached, and I felt emotionally drained, but it felt good to get out of the car and stretch my legs. There were no signs of civilization in viewing distance, other than farm buildings. I felt safe that we were isolated—surrounded only by nature.

Max rushed us into the farmhouse. Once he locked the door, Max said, "Don't turn on the lights. And stay quiet if you hear any noise other than me. I'll always identify myself, so you know it's safe."

He had us stand by the door while he found a flashlight. The farmhouse had electricity and inside running water. It was also equipped for power outages with a hand-pump well and an outhouse. "Don't use the outhouse. Don't leave the house. Until I can get your family here and we can figure out what we're going to do, stay in the cellar and handle your needs down there. It has a sink and a water faucet."

As I descended the stairs, I lost my footing and cascaded down the last three steps. Ben rushed to me, "You okay, Helen?" He helped me up.

"Yes," I laughed. "It's these darn shoes." We were in such a hurry to get out of the car and into the house that I hadn't taken the time to remove any of Max's clothes.

Max shined the flashlight on me, and we all laughed. "That padding saved you." He helped me take off the coat and hat.

Laughing felt good; we needed it.

Max was able to light one of the lanterns without worrying about revealing our secret location because the basement had no windows and the door was closed. It was at that point he revealed in greater detail what he had seen and heard that set our rescue in motion. "The dispatch said that Jewish shops and synagogues were to be destroyed."

"What about the men being rounded up in trucks?" I asked.

"Those Jewish men are being transported to concentration camps."

"Why!" I cried. "The men attacking those innocent people didn't look like the SS. They were in suits."

Max shook his head. "The men in suits causing all the destruction were the SS, Helen." He swallowed hard and pressed his hands to his stomach. I was worried he might be ill. He went on to explain Hitler's directions to Goebbels. "To avoid a backlash against his police state, Hitler wanted all attacks to look like German citizens were rising up against Jews."

Ben stood silent. Tears running down his pale face.

Years later, I learned that over a hundred Jews were killed during the night of hell, *Kristallnacht* (the Night of Broken Glass). Thousands of Jewish shops and hundreds of synagogues were vandalized and destroyed. In total, 30,000 men were rounded up, leaving their wives and children to fend for themselves.

Would knowing the truth have helped me while I was still on the street in the midst of the violence? I doubt it. Nothing could have changed the horror and repulsion I felt over witnessing the unconscionable. It would not change what had happened to any of the poor victims I'd seen.

Max, bless his sweet heart, in an attempt to redirect our attention off the overwhelming tragedy, had us look around the cellar. The room that served as our hiding place was large—almost as big as his apartment. I assumed that the rest of the farmhouse was spacious as well. There was no furniture, but there were plenty of blankets, pillows, wooden crates, gardening tools, and a few metal trunks. At the far end, away from the stairs, was a large, deep enamel sink. Shelves surrounding the room were filled with a supply of canned goods. In a corner next to the sink was a large stack of cut wood for the upstairs fireplace. Max looked at the provisions and put down the bag he brought. "I didn't know we had so much food here. That's good. But you'll need to ration, especially with your whole family here."

When he mentioned my family, anxiety gripped my stomach. "Please be careful with my father. His health is not good."

Max smiled as he handed me the flashlight. "I'll do my best." He hugged Ben and me, and said, "Whatever happens, stay down here! Do not go outside! And do not make any noise! Keep your supplies hidden so the room looks deserted. And if you suspect danger, hide behind that stack of wood."

Ben, who had been uncharacteristically quiet since we arrived, said, "We will. Thank you, Max. Please be careful."

Max nodded and said to me, "Hold the light on the steps for me."

We watched him leave and heard him lock the front door. As the sound of his truck moved out of earshot, I prayed that my parents would be safe. And I prayed that Max would find them in time.

The Seven Year Dress

Chapter Twelve

Like crippled, wounded soldiers trudging through snow with heavy hearts, we slogged our way through the various items in the cellar, trying to make our new (hopefully temporary) "home" as comfortable as possible. The wood floor was damp, so we used canvas tarpaulins we found to cover the floor. We put blankets and pillows on top of the tarpaulins to make our beds. Assessing our pitiful sleeping accommodations, Ben said, "We can sleep in our coats."

"Yes, it's so cold," I replied. The temperature must have dipped down to what felt like the mid-20s.

Ben, being the considerate brother—always looking out for me—asked, "Are you okay? Do you need to talk?"

My heart was heavy. My mind was a tornado of images, both remembered and fabricated. None of them were comforting. My body twitched and trembled from fear. My shoulders were so tense, I felt pulled back a foot. I looked at my brother with tears welling in my eyes. I was exhausted and didn't want to deplete myself further by breaking down crying. I distracted myself by looking around the room at crates and the shelves. I was also too drained to want to relive what I had seen, and I didn't want to talk about the abhorrent feelings that wouldn't leave me alone. Right now it was best I try to keep busy. "Not now, Ben," I sighed." I think we should see what we have. You know, get ready for Papa, Mamma, Lawrence, and Shana."

"I understand," said Ben as he surveyed the cans of food. "Borden's milk, Nescafe, ginger ale." He listed off some of the items he saw.

"Any vegetables or protein—like meat or cheese?" I waited while he foraged through the provisions.

"Yes, a few cans of tinned meat. And lima and kidney beans, sweet corn, sauerkraut, tomatoes, peas, Maggi cubes, and," he shook a can, "soup." His finger moved over several more cans. "Lots of soup."

"Okay, that's good. Looks like what we have could feed our entire family for a couple of weeks."

"There's more," he said as his foot kicked a big burlap sack. "Rice, but how can we cook it?"

"We'll figure out a way. We could light a small fire or mix it in with some of the soup. I'm just glad there's hearty food to help us stay healthy until we're moved from here."

"Do you know where?" Ben's eyes squinted concern.

"No. I only know that Max said once he brings the rest of our family here, he'd figure out what the next step is. He'll probably find us a place to relocate to. He'll be back soon, and then we'll know."

"I hope everything works out." Ben shook his head. "I'm worried about—"

"I trust Max!" I raised my voice and, with unconvincing force, said, "We'll be fine."

"I know you want to believe that, Helen, but…" Ben's cheek muscle tightened into a spasm.

"Yes, I want to believe that. It makes me feel better. What's wrong with that? How about you entertaining a positive outcome as well?" Putting a hand on his arm and gently pressing. "Please Ben, what good is worrying about something that hasn't happened. Soon we'll all be together."

He grabbed for and squeezed my hand. "You're right, sis. I love you."

"I love you too. Okay, then, how about we finish the inventory?" I smiled.

I took a look at the supplies Max had packed and was happy to find toothpaste and a few toothbrushes, a hairbrush, a mirror, and some deodorant. Also included was a battery-powered radio. "Ben, a radio. Max gave us a radio." My voice raised a decibel with excitement.

Ben came to look at it. "This is good." He picked it up and turned it over. "It uses a lead-acid, wet cell…"

"Huh?"

"The battery," he said, pointing to it. "The only problem is it needs to be recharged every few days."

I laughed.

Ben tilted his head sideways. "What are you laughing at?"

"I wouldn't say that's our only problem."

Smiling, Ben said, "Good point."

It felt good to have those moments of normalcy: smiling, laughing, and expressing our love for each other.

"Ah, problem solved. Look," he pointed to a gas-powered generator that could be used to charge it. "It'll give us a way to listen to the radio, to hear the news."

I felt relief. It amazed me that something so apparently small as being able to stay informed made me feel better. It meant a lot to me. I felt a deep sense of gratitude that, after all the horrifying events I'd seen and the fear I had about the future of my country, my will to live and survive remained strong.

Feeling a little more hopeful after finding the food and the radio, I allowed myself to relax. That's when exhaustion overwhelmed me. I lay down on my makeshift bed. The minute my body hit the blanket, I fell asleep. My last thought before I drifted off was hoping I'd awaken to my family's arrival.

A loud noise startled me out of my sound sleep. In my groggy, disoriented state, I didn't know if it was real or nightmare. Looking at the wristwatch I was wearing, I realized I had been asleep a few hours. I heard another sound; it was coming from somewhere outside. At first, I was excited that Max had arrived with my family. I waited quietly, as he instructed. When no one entered the farmhouse in what felt like ten minutes, I started to panic. "Ben." I shoved his shoulder to rouse him from a sound sleep. "Wake up. Someone's outside."

"Let me sleep," he mumbled.

I shook him harder. "Ben," I whispered right into his ear, "get up! There's a noise outside."

"Fine, all right." He stirred and sat up. "What's going on?"

"Listen." I barely breathed the word.

"I don't hear anything."

"There's someone out there. Give it a minute."

The clattering of garbage cans got Ben's attention. He jumped up and ran to the side of the cellar where the sound seemed closest. He put his ear to the wall, but he shook his head, indicating that it wasn't helping. I watched as he took out his pocketknife and carefully plied a knot in the wooden wall. The sounds grew louder while he worked the piece loose. The edge popped up, and we could see through the wall; the view was limited, but we now had a way to discern day from night. We could see outside.

Ben peered through the hole, and his shoulders relaxed. He moved aside to let me have a look. The commotion outside was not Max, but a bear rummaging through the trash cans.

The excitement made it impossible for me to get back to sleep. I was on edge again—continuing to check my wristwatch, imagining all kinds of dangers as I listened to the howling wind and animals scurrying around outside. When the sun came in through the hole in the wall, I became even more anxious. Max had had plenty of time to drive to Berlin and return with the rest of my family. By the time my brother opened his eyes, I was pacing the room.

"What time is it?" he asked.

Looking at my watch for the millionth time, I sighed, "A little after ten."

"What? I slept for over eight hours." He stretched. "I can't believe it."

"Me neither. I've been up for hours. Ben, they should have been here by now. I'm really worried."

He leaned over to grab the bag that Max had packed from his kitchen. "Bread." He smiled. "You must be hungry." He sorted through other packages and found some cooked sausage wrapped in foil. He rolled one in a piece of bread and handed it to me. "Eat this."

I was too worried to eat. "I'll just have some water." I went to the sink and cupped my hands to drink.

"You need to eat to stay healthy."

"You sound like Papa."

"Yes, I do. And he would tell you to stop fretting and eat." He bit into his sandwich. "It's good, Helen."

He was right. I made myself eat. And I tried to get my attention from the niggling feeling in my bones that something was wrong.

When two days had passed, I was sick with fear for Max and my family. "Something's happened to them," I lamented to Ben.

Ben kept saying, "It'll be fine. It hasn't been that long, Helen."

My ears heard one thing, but my body sensed another. A prickly feeling traveled from my head to my toes; it was as if my fear was crawling under my skin. I couldn't rest or eat properly. I tried to squelch horrifying images of the SS brutalizing my parents, Lawrence and Shana the same way I had seen them attack all those innocent people on the street. *Oh God, please let them be safe. Max, please bring them to us.* Unbridled thoughts of fire, destruction and death filled in my head. I picked at the skin around my fingernails till they bled.

Opening a can of soup with a can opener Max packed for us, Ben asked, "Do you think it would help you to talk about what happened that night?"

"I already told you, no."

"It may help to talk…"

"It's not going to help, Ben! How can talking help? It won't bring back the dead or repair the damage to property. It won't bring back all the disrupted families and ruined lives!"

"Quiet!" he whispered. "You're getting too loud."

My scalp ached with frustration. I clutched the top of my head. "I don't care!" I shouted.

He grabbed me and covered my mouth with his hand. "Yes, you do. And so do I. Now stop acting like a child. We have to stay alive and not expose this hiding place."

In the dim light of our lantern, I could see beads of sweat on Ben's forehead. My fit of hysteria had gravely worried my dear brother. I softly stroked his arm, and when he released his hand, I broke into crying.

Ben spoke slowly, calmly. "That's good. Let it out. However you can, let it out. But do it quietly."

"I'm sorry. I'm sorry. Please forgive me." I sobbed and continued to sob intermittently for two days. Finally, I said, "They're dead. I know it. I feel it."

"Helen, be patient. We were both there that night, so you know as well as I do that Max could have been unable to get away.

Please God, let it be that. This was our only hope.

The Seven Year Dress

Chapter Thirteen

I paced and worried about why it was taking so long for Max to return to us. Horrible thoughts ran through my head. Much later, I learned what actually happened while we waited for my family in that cellar. The destructive consequences of Hitler's wrath over the German diplomat's assassination in Paris continued to spiral out of control. As if destroying businesses, homes and families weren't punishment enough, Hitler fined the Jewish community one billion Reichsmarks for vom Rath's murder. He demanded another six million Reichmarks for property damage to be paid to the state.

And a missive was sent to Goebbels, which he read in part at a meeting. "I have received a letter written on the Fuehrer's orders requesting that the Jewish question be now, once and for all, coordinated and solved one way or another...I implore competent agencies to take all measures for the elimination of the Jew from the German economy..." The purpose of that meeting with the high-ranking Nazi leaders was to make the Jews responsible for

Kristallnacht. It set in motion laws to totally remove the Jews from the economy.

The era of voluntary Aryanization had ended, and the era of forced Aryanization had begun. Jews were to turn over precious metal to the Reich. Pensions were reduced from civil service jobs. Bonds, stocks, jewelry, and artwork were confiscated. Driver's licenses were suspended. Radios were seized. Laws pertaining to tenants no longer applied to Jews. A curfew was set to keep Jews off the streets between 9:00 p.m. and 5:00 a.m. in the summer and 8:00 p.m. and 6:00 a.m. in the winter. And to ensure that the Jews could not retaliate, regulations were issued against them owning or carrying weapons and ammunition; they were ordered to surrender all firearms to the local police authority. Immediately. It was a devastatingly dangerous time of public humiliation and degradation for the subjugated Jews in Germany and other German occupied territories. The path that would ultimately lead to Hitler's Final Solution had been set and put in motion.

I doubt that knowing any of this while in the basement with Ben would have mattered. All that I cared about was the safe arrival of my parents, Lawrence, and Shana.

Two days moved into three, and we continued to wait. With my attention riveted on my watch, I obsessed over the fate of my family. I picked at my fingers, my legs, and dry moles on my arms. My oozing, raw skin bled as my unabated nervousness—and bad habit of digging into my flesh—worsened. I was distracted only by Ben's deathly pale appearance. When his body started to shake, I felt his forehead. "Ben, you're burning up." Frantically trying to find something to soak in water, I resorted to my undergarment. I saturated a pair of underpants with cold water from the tap and applied the makeshift compress to his face. Remembering that Max had left us with supplies from his apartment, I rummaged through his bags, hoping to find aspirins. There were none. We had no medication of any sort.

Although it was cold in the cellar, Ben's clothes were soaked with sweat. I feared he would dehydrate if I couldn't get fluids in him. I opened a can of soup. "Here," I handed it to him. "Drink this."

"I feel nauseated." He pushed it away.

"We're a stubborn lot, aren't we?" I smiled. "Just force it down and if you vomit, you vomit."

"Water," he grunted.

"Ben, you need something with salt in it." I remembered from a first aid class in school about how sodium in salt helps keep fluids in the body, especially when in shock. He wasn't in shock, but I feared he could head in that direction.

As sick as he was, he smiled and said, "You're a pest."

I laughed. He was right. When I wanted my way, I was a nuisance. My eyes welled up with tears as I recalled my mother saying, *don't be a pest,* when I'd bother her. Being strong-headed may have helped me then with Ben, but it sure hadn't helped me win friends in school. Aside from my family, Max, and Isaac, I'd been a loner. I had to wonder if it was because of my bullheadedness. What was happening now—being in hiding and the reason for it, being stigmatized a Jew—was degrading. For the first time in my life, I felt helplessly out of control, and I despised Hitler and all his vile puppets. No self-righteousness or assertive protestations could change any of it.

The sound of Ben slurping the soup made me feel better. I hated that sound when we were at the table having meals, but now it was music to my ears. "How's the nausea?"

"Not as bad." He looked up at me standing over him.

"Finish it, and I'll get you some water." I kept plying him with water to drink and continued to moisten the cloth on his forehead as soon as it became warm. Tending to Ben brought back memories of when we were younger and home from school. Sick. First, one would catch something and then, one by one, the whole family went down. My mother cared for us with chicken soup and loving attention. I ached for her attentiveness now—her eyes upon us and her soft words, always comforting us through the worst of fevers, coughs, aches and pains. I saw her beautiful face in my mind's eye. Whenever I envisioned my dear mother, my father was always close to her, love for his wife radiating from him. I wanted what they had. They touched each other with gentle pats on the back. My father would tenderly move a strand of hair from her face. Their simple gestures were made with warmth and compassion. Although the pressure of making a life together sometimes brought out anger and frustration, I loved my family and wouldn't change a thing about them for all the money in the world.

Ben's ashen-like skin took on a pinker glow, and I thought he might be getting better. He certainly looked like he had more life in him. Life. The idea reminded me of my father's words: *Life is precious. It is the most important thing.* How right he was. It was then I made a silent vow to do whatever I must to stay alive.

Breathing a sigh of relief that Ben looked more like himself, I covered him with all the blankets and turned off the lantern. Wearing two coats, I nodded off only to be reawakened by his tossing and turning. Ben's body was trembling, and he had developed a gurgling cough. When he sat up to try to catch his breath, he hyperventilated. I panicked. Unsure of what to do, I patted his back, hoping to clear the rattling and wheezing coming from his lungs. I could feel the beat of my pounding heart. My chest hurt as I watched his efforts to take in air. I hoped he wasn't dying. Finally, his breathing slowed; so did my heartbeats. When he fell back to sleep, I wiped a pool of sweat off my face.

Poor Ben! Too much had happened. The war on Jews. Worry about our family and Max and this cold, damp basement. No wonder he got sick. I stayed up with him as he slept fitfully, tossing and turning. Finally, a few hours later, he relaxed into a snoring slumber.

I was not able to rest that night as disturbing images returned. Men in suits and the SA in their brown shirts during that night of hell kept coming back to me with my unanswered question, *why?* Why did the paramilitary help the SS? They were local Germans, so why would they destroy property and neighborhoods? Why would they go along with killing Jews? I was not raised to believe in or understand evil. What Jewish child is prepared for a world where a monstrous man exists who wants to kill Jews? To that vicious, dictatorial despot, a drop of Jewish blood was a death sentence. The question *why* reverberated in my head until it hurt. I felt like I was going to throw up.

Watching my vulnerable, innocent, loving brother sleep, I realized that evil has no explanation. Hitler's profoundly immoral and malevolent actions were as much of a mystery to me as the alchemy of love. The fact that good German people were falling under his spell of hatred was even more confounding to me. Like it or not, I had to accept that depravity exists. But my father gave my siblings and me an antidote to this kind of poison. He taught us that life, and living a life of peace and kindness, is what's most important. I needed to keep my focus on staying alive and keeping my family alive, no matter what. And no matter how. And, somehow in the process, maintaining my humanity.

Daylight came, and, with it, Ben's fever broke. That day there was something to be grateful for. I hoped it would also be the day my family would arrive.

Chapter Fourteen

The day proceeded, and, although Ben was coughing up some yellow gunk, his fever didn't return. Worried that, as night approached, he might take a turn for the worse, I suggested we sneak upstairs to look for medication. I also wanted to see if there was a phone to try to contact our family.

Ben pushed the palm of his hand out in front of me. "No! Helen. Stay put. We're going to do what Max told us to do."

"What about your cough?" I pleaded. "If it gets worse…"

"I feel better," he croaked. "Um. Right now, I'm okay. Let's just leave it at that."

To avoid aggravating him more, I yielded. But I insisted on continuing to force fluids down his throat. "I'll agree to this if you don't fight me over drinking liquids."

"You're going to make me use up all the rations," he joked about the multiple cans of soup I made him eat.

"Very funny, Ben," I gave his arm a gentle smack. We were always playful—teasing each other. Although I loved

Lawrence and Shana, Ben was my favorite sibling. He was closest to my age, four years older, plus we had a friendship with Max in common. My other siblings never took to Max like we did. And vice versa. I also suspected that Max had a crush on Ben, so handsome with his big, dark-brown eyes and infectious smile.

For the twentieth time, I scrounged the cellar looking for anything I might have overlooked that could help Ben. For the twentieth time, I found nothing new. I noticed the radio on top of the workbench, and, for the first time since Ben became ill, I thought of turning it on.

The brown wood surface was smooth and cool to the touch. In the upper right corner under a glass covering, I saw the dial of channels. Two knobs were below the dial: one for turning it on and volume, and the other for stations. The sound came from the left face of the box, which was covered by a thick-meshed beige material and small wood slats. I hesitated, hoping it wouldn't give me bad news. Ben must have sensed my misgivings. He threw a balled up sock at me. "What are you waiting for?"

"What if it's all horrible news? Do we really want to know?" In the last several days, I'd grown accustomed to feeling anxious and wary. If I had to survive, I knew I could. I had settled into an aberrant version of comfort down in that cellar with Ben, and didn't want to disturb it. Picking a pimple on my cheek, I checked the radio, "Let's hold off." I looked back at him. "I don't want any unsettling news to make you feel worse."

"Me?" He sat up straight. "I want to know. You're the one that's a bundle of nerves. Look at you." He motioned to my hands and arms. "You're plucking your skin off."

Feeling self-conscious, I pulled my sleeves down to cover as much of my body as possible. "You really want to find out what's happening...out there?"

Coughing, he nodded yes.

I turned the radio on.

Static.

"Try changing the channel." Ben cleared his throat.

I moved the dial slightly to the right.

More static.

"It could be our location or the atmosphere affecting the signal." Ben was the handyman. He was good with equipment: radios, cars, and appliances. I had a newfound appreciation for what he and Lawrence had done to bring in extra cash.

"Anything we can do to make it work better?" I asked.

"Move it to different locations." Ben's words slowed with pauses in between. He took in a slow, tired breath. "Or just wait for the weather to change."

I picked up the radio and moved around the basement, but all we heard were crackles. Nothing discernible. "Not a thing."

"Leave it for now. At least we know it has juice."

Frustrated that I couldn't get the darn radio to work and observing my tired brother, I let it go.

As the hours passed and Ben slept, I busied myself making a mental inventory of our food and supplies. I peered outside through the tiny hole in the wall at the unspoiled countryside when the inventory was complete. My life in the cellar was a soothing contrast to the chaotic Berlin I left days before. The weather was cold, but the bright sun shining through leaves and forest plants warmed my body. I knew that waterways and lakes surrounded Brandenburg. We were in a fertile place for farmland and growing potatoes, turnips, and asparagus. I yearned to be outside walking among the birch, pine, and Scotch fir trees. Feeling the soft earth beneath my feet would have been heavenly. I imagined being in a greenhouse spreading mulch over my flower garden, and growing tomatoes. If I had a farm, I'd have sheep and cattle. My family would drink fresh milk every day.

A noise outside interrupted my daydreaming. A doe with two fawns moved past a tree and into my line of vision. The mother guiding her timid young and watching over them reminded me of Mamma. Heartache overwhelmed me as they walked away. My chest felt too heavy to take in a proper breath. Wracked with grief, I wanted to break down the basement wall, run to Berlin, and find my family. I wanted to feel their arms around me so I could soothe the ache inside of me—the one that refused to leave. Finally, the dike burst and out came the deluge of all the tears I had been suppressing. I sat on one of the wood boxes and wept my heart out.

The labyrinth of emotions that I didn't want to feel, experience, or face—fear, anger, and unbearable loss—enveloped me. I reached out in desperation like a helpless baby who needed her mommy. *Hold me. Comfort me. Tell me that everything will be fine. Where are you?* By the time the oceans of deep sorrow moved through me, it was nightfall.

Not sleepy, nor even tired, I shuffled around with a dim lantern looking for something to take my attention off my torment, to occupy my restless mind. I found some coal in a bag against one wall. I broke off a piece and grabbed a small, flat board from the pile of firewood to use to draw on. Images of flames, of shattered glass, and of crying babies sprang from my hand. Screams, anger, hostility and hatred were exorcised from my soul as I drew scenes of the agony I felt. Magically, I started to entertain ideas of hope. Could my parents be safe? Could they be hiding somewhere tending to Lawrence and Shana? Had they escaped and was Max looking for them? A promising reflection of light shined from the lantern as I continued my scribbling with the black chalk.

At around 9:00 p.m., I felt sleepy. Ben was snoring by my side as I closed my eyes. In the dark early morning, hours away from dawn, the sound of tires on gravel woke me from a sound sleep. I sat up, nudged Ben, and in a hushed tone said, "Someone's here!" I got up and went to the peephole. The moonlight was bright enough to reveal what looked like Max's truck moving around to the back of the farmhouse.

Ben stirred awake and looked at me.

We held our breath until the movement outside stopped.

The front door opened.

We held our breath again.

Footsteps on the floor above us.

We waited. No speaking. No breathing.

The door to the cellar opened and shut while a familiar voice said, "It's Max."

The Seven Year Dress

Chapter Fifteen

Max came down the stairs and shuffled toward us carrying two large suitcases. His uniform smelled like decaying flesh. I felt my heart pounding in my ears. A chill ran up my spine. He was a vision of something I barely recognized. He looked as if he was fifty-nine, not nineteen, years old. His eyes were sunken and had dark baggy circles under them; a crop of new wrinkles carved deep worry lines across his once unmarred face. He didn't have to say a word to tell me his news was bad. His sorrowful, weary expression, his dirty, unkempt hair, hunched shoulders, and his arms glued to his sides spoke for him.

"What's that nauseating smell?" asked Ben from his makeshift bed, the rosy coloring leaving his cheeks.

Time felt like a sinkhole of slowly eroding soil. I feared that the minute Max told us the horrible truth he wore all over his body, that we'd plummet beyond retrieval.

"Ben, you don't look well." Max avoided Ben's question. "Here, I brought you these." He put down the suitcases. "Some of your clothes and other—"

"Max!" I hissed, interrupting him. "Where are our parents? Where's the rest of our family?"

Max bowed his head and sniffed back tears. When he barely mumbled, "I'm so sorry…" I lost it and screamed, "Tell us what happened!"

"I had to wait to return here. Security is very tight. Everyone is being watched and the slightest suspicion…I didn't want to compromise you two. Not after," Max stopped, evading what he obviously didn't want to reveal.

My patience gone, I screamed. "Tell us what happened!"

"Shush, Helen, lower the volume," pleaded Ben.

Max's breathy, brittle voice was hardly discernible. "There's no easy way to say this."

"Just say it!" I demanded.

"Your parents are dead."

"Dead?" I gasped.

"What?" Ben reacted.

"It can't be." I choked. "You're joking. Right? This is a bad joke?" Shocked, feeling as if I was being electrocuted, my nervous system sent convulsions to my muscles. I couldn't stop shaking. I saw Max's mouth move; I even heard the words he said. But now my mind was muddling up everything as if this whole scene was playing out under water, and Max's words—therefore, my understanding of them—were garbled. Wrong. They couldn't be true. But there was no way Max would joke about something this important. "Where are Lawrence and Shana?" I asked.

"Lawrence is dead."

"No," I cried. "Nooo!"

"Shana?" Ben's voice cracked as he wiped his eyes dry.

"Missing." Max stood, frozen with pain, straining to find the words to describe our worst nightmare. Inch by excruciating inch, he managed to tell us what had happened to our family.

When Max returned from dropping us off at the farm, Jewish men were being round up for deportation to concentration camps. He went to my parents' home. The Gestapo was already in the neighborhood. SS and the brown shirt SA were marching on the street. Nazi flags were being hung from windows. An SS officer spotted Max and ordered him to help carry out Goebbels's orders. He had no choice but to join in. Breaking down door after door, the Nazi's and their sympathizers uprooted Jews. Screams were silenced with gunshots, and protesters were beaten to within an inch of their lives. At gunpoint, husbands trudged into to the trucks, leaving behind their wives and children.

Max had learned that Jewish men and women bearing forenames of non-Jewish origin had to add "Israel" and "Sara," respectively, to their first names. All Jews were obliged to carry identity cards that indicated their Jewish heritage. Furthermore, all Jewish passports had to be stamped with an identifying letter "J". The Reich designed these measures to separate Jews from the rest of the public. "They went into your home," his pupils dilated as he looked at Ben and me, "to verify that the changes had been made to their papers, passports and…" His entire body shook with grief.

My mouth went dry. I tried to swallow a lump in my throat that felt like a boulder. "And?" I sighed.

"Your father and Lawrence were escorted out first. They were quiet, obedient. Then Lawrence said something like, 'why?'" Max looked away. I saw his lower lip trembling so much that I didn't think he would be able to say anything else. But he made a gulping sound, wiped his eyes and nose with his sleeve, and said quickly, "Bullets. Someone started shooting…to punish Lawrence. Your father. Killed, too. Crossfire." He covered his face with his hands.

"Papa," I lamented. "Lawrence." A pain carved into my chest.

"What happened to Mamma?" Ben whispered his question.

Max uncovered his face. He looked ruined, drained of all emotion. "She walked out into the street and ran to them. The SS screamed orders to the SA. She was shot in the back as she held your father." Max took in a slow breath. "I'm so sorry." His pained expression pierced my gut.

As I listened to this horror story, my body trembled. It hadn't fully sunk in yet. My mind was incapable of grasping that any part of what Max had told us was true. I simply couldn't imagine living in a world without my parents and two of my siblings. "You said Shana is missing?" My voice broke.

Exhausted, Max nodded.

Ben asked, "Where is she?" His head was bent forward as if too heavy to lift. The front of his shirt was dark where too many tears had fallen.

"I don't know." Max paused. "I tried to find out. I looked at relocation lists...I don't know where she is."

"Perhaps she got away?" Ben looked up. He spoke as if he were bargaining with Max for Shana's safety.

"I hope so," said Max. But his diverted eyes told me differently. If she had tried to flee, she would have been shot.

"No, this can't be." I moaned. I paced. I grabbed a can of soup and threw it across the room. "This isn't happening." Still reeling in shocked denial, I insisted, "It can't be true."

Persecution and hatred had walked through the door to my soul and ripped out my heart. From that day on, I lived in the terror that anything I loved or bonded with could be destroyed. The only threads connecting me to this life were my brother Ben, my friendship with Max, and the hope that my sister was alive and safe. I was consumed with dread that this devastating news would worsen my brother's illness. If he developed pneumonia and died, what would I do? And what about Max? He witnessed what his people did to my people. Had this changed him? *No, no! I can't think that way. He has more to hide than I do. I won't think that way! Breathe. Breathe.* I calmed the frenzy I was thinking myself into and swore I would rest in the belief that Max was my friend.

I was always the inquisitive child in our family. Now, I hated the word *why!* Lawrence asked "why" and the Nazis killed him. Papa, too. And Mamma. Simply wanting to understand was now punishable by death! From that simple, innocent question on that horrible day, the world had grown dark and cold. The Age of Enlightenment was dead.

Finally, there was nothing left to say, and all that remained were frayed emotions in desperate need of soothing. No one in the cellar was able to offer a balm to heal our wounded hearts, and we all seemed to know it.

Max noted that daylight was not far from dawning. He had to travel back to Berlin to report to his SS job by 9:00 a.m. "I can't attract attention to myself. Keeping you both safe is my only priority now." Before leaving, he tried to lift our spirits by showing us some of the things he brought: chocolate, cookies, books and clothing he had obtained from our home. None of it touched my mood: heartbroken to the core.

In a forlorn tone that was barely audible, he said, "Stay strong, and please don't do anything foolish. I beg you to stay put. I'll get back as soon as I'm able to. I'll do what I can to find out about Shana." With that, he walked out. Moments later, the loud engine and the sound of tires spitting up gravel faded into the distance.

Ben and I were left in damp, silent sorrow. I was sickened by what Max told us. How could an entire nation be legitimately handed over to a group of malignant, sadistic, dictatorial murderers? These villainous puppets of Hitler were trained to hunt and kill men, women, and children. I couldn't bear to think of the guiltless who were condemned to extermination without any chance of escaping their fate. How could a human being degrade, humiliate, and torture another human? The victims were robbed of their dignity. They were deprived of their strength to resist, and even the will to live. Where was their torturers' remorse? Where do the emotions of these heartless men reside? And how could innocents try to escape their demise by joining the villains in the slaughter of fellow countrymen by betraying them to the Nazis?

What makes people sell themselves into slavery like this? And where is the God that allows such atrocities to happen?

Chapter Sixteen

Time moved sluggishly as days blurred together while I focused on helping Ben. Overwhelmed by the stress from terrible news, Ben's health slid backward. His cough worsened. His fever returned. I feared he'd lose his will to live, and I had to do something. I couldn't lose him, too. All my life, I could depend on Ben to keep me centered when I'd go to pieces. He kept me from falling apart down in that cold, lonely cellar. After Max had told us our parents and Lawrence were dead, Ben went downhill. Now it was my turn to be the uplifting, stabilizing force in his precious life.

He'd just finished the soup I forced him to eat when I asked, "Would you like me to read aloud from one of the books Max brought?" Along with some chocolate candy, food, and our clothing, Max brought three of my books: *Babbitt* by Sinclair Lewis, *The Great Gatsby* by F. Scott Fitzgerald, and a newer one, *Of Mice and Men* by John Steinbeck. I was particularly enamored with the American authors of the 1920s and early 1930s. I thought reading

161

something to him might be useful to uplift us. In the past, reading had helped me escape. We both needed to flee mentally from our situation, which was flooded with loss and sorrow.

Hardly able to lift his head, and exhausted from hacking up phlegm through the night, he shook his head in protest.

"Do it for me?" I begged.

He managed a weak whisper, "That's what you used to get me to eat the soup." He half-smiled. "Once a pest, always a pest."

Finally, one of my bad habits worked in my favor. It appeared to be working for him too. "Maybe being a pest isn't always a bad thing." I nudged him with my elbow.

My older brother rolled his eyes.

"Ben," I persisted. "Max brought some good books."

"You're not going to let me rest in peace," he panted.

He wasn't joking. And it struck a nerve. We existed in a morose fog of disbelief, for the most part, without smiles or laughter in that dank cellar. But as reality was beginning to set in, and as he regained enough strength, I dared to speak one overarching truth shredding my core. "Ben, I'm scared."

His rheumy eyes met mine, and I knew from his expression that he understood. "I'll be all right, sis."

"I don't want to lose you...too."

I didn't read to him that day, but we did communicate. I spoke to him; he nodded or puffed a few words. Conversations invariably tracked to topics we didn't intend to discuss or even want to consider. At first, we focused on Max and the enormous risk he took by hiding us. Our mutual fears about living in hiding, and the constant worry of being discovered by the enemy kept us busy talking about precautions: keeping the lantern light dim at night, being vigilant about silence, and staying confined to the basement. Ben was adamant about not going upstairs. The danger was too great.

After about a week of fitful sleep, Ben's cough subsided, and the thick, gooey, green secretions became clear mucus. I breathed easier now that Ben was breathing easier. But as Ben's physical health continued to improve, my mood darkened. I felt as if I had been thrown down a deep well. Ben was having none of my despondency, sluggishness, and unwillingness to engage with him. He spoke firmly with a strong command when he asserted, "Helen, you need to snap out of it." He went to a large container that we used for elimination and urinated. "What do you think our parents would say to us while we mope around, burning daylight, wallowing in self-pity?"

"How dare you? Self-pity? I'm grieving a terrible loss. I can't just turn off a switch for the pain to go away. I can't! And I won't!"

"Too stubborn to let it go?" He wiggled himself to let out the last drop of urine. Turning to me with a smile, he said, "How about we help each other? You don't think my heart is broken, forever damaged property? It is. But we're here now, alive. We need to make that mean something."

Ben's voice morphed into my father's, and, once again, I heard those familiar words: *life is precious.* But my ache was too deep. I wanted to hold on to my pain to avenge the deaths of my family members—to return their hatred back to the monsters who began this nightmare. The time would come when I could do something about it. Then my mother's sweet voice came to me: *you are taking the poison of hatred and hoping it will kill them.* I realized that what I do to them, I'm doing to myself. My parents' wisdom crystalized for me at that moment, as obvious as the bright morning sun lighting up the once dark sky. I knew then that I had to breathe in something stronger than the acrimony. I had to replace these feelings of hatred and revenge with gratitude. Letting go of the hostility was my only way to have a life worth living. Could I transform the traumatic hurt into something good for me? *Gratitude? What does it really mean? How can something so elusive supplant the tangible agony I feel?* I whispered softly, "Mamma," as if to beckon her.

Remembering Mamma brought a crooked smile to my face and a glow that warmed my cold arms and legs. I envisioned my mother laughing in the kitchen when she caught us stealing cookie dough from her mixing bowl. I saw her rushing to us when we'd burn our hands on the hot baking tray. There was a lot of love in my family; plenty to be remembered when we needed it. As if at their funerals, Ben and I spent time reminiscing about silly, fun family antics that made us smile. As the memories permeated us, laughter returned.

I found gratitude in that basement. My heartache never stopped, but I learned to be grateful for the essentials of life: for the air in my lungs, the visions my eyes behold, and the very experience of being alive. It was in that cellar with Ben that I gained a firsthand appreciation for the resilience of the human spirit. All thanks to Max, who gave me a safe hiding place and the gift of life.

Although we could not confirm it, we imagined there must be a network of underground efforts to help Jews. I felt sure that there were others out there like Max, risking everything to help others. Reflecting on the worst in the human condition also highlights the best. "I believe there are more good people than bad ones in this world," I said to my brother.

"Of course, there are. Only a few bad apples…"

"You and your metaphors," I smiled.

"Hey, if that made you smile, I've got a few more up my sleeve."

"Spare me," I joked back. My healing had begun with the contemplation of good people in the world. It was a mirror that our parents held up to us, to see the best of the human condition despite reasons and temptations to look at darker elements. To emulate them gave meaning to my existence.

Chapter Seventeen

Another day, another week, another month went by, and I still struggled with turbulent emotions. I felt helpless when unbearable grief or blinding anger smothered me, but then light banter with my brother nearly always pulled me back to feeling better about life. I had made a big ball out of a bundle of dirty clothes for use as a punching bag when the anger returned.

Ben and I were good company for each other. When I was down, he was up, and vice versa. We balanced each other. Chattering, mostly mindless blathering, kept us occupied. We were never able to get the radio to work. We must have been out of all stations' distance ranges. I never succumbed to my urge to take it upstairs to see if it would work up there. While our confinement and absence of news were frustrating, we never lost sight of what we imagined was going on in the outside world.

As winter melted into spring, then summer, and into the autumn of 1939, we approached our first anniversary in the cellar. Max had continued his regular visits in the middle of the night every couple of weeks. He brought more food: bread, vegetables, and fruit. He came with bags of potatoes. Using the wood down there, we built small, contained fires to cook them.

He also brought more bleach for us to clean our toilet bucket and rinse our waste down the sink. That simple act of kindness prevented us from getting intestinal problems or whatever other sicknesses come from exposure to human urine and feces. Although both Ben and I suffered from bouts of nausea and vomiting, we never had diarrhea. I attributed our upset stomachs and retching to being nervous so much of the time.

Max also brought news about current events that we craved to know. Without a radio or newspaper, I ached for information about what was happening in the world outside the basement. Max wasted no time giving us the highlights. Hitler had invaded Poland. Since Britain and France were legally bound by a treaty to help Poland, they declared war on Germany. World War II had started. He also mentioned that he had convinced his parents, Ludwig and Ela, not to come to the farm during the past year due to the unrest in society, and now, due to the increased danger of civilians traveling during wartime, they agreed to stay away from the farm during the war.

"Oh, that's good news, Max." Although I hated the idea of war, I felt hopeful that the Allies would stop the atrocities, and we would be free to find Shana. Max hadn't had any luck finding her.

"No, I'm afraid it's not good news." Max frowned as he spoke.

I had jumped to the wrong conclusion and assumed the result was favorable when, in fact, it was just the opposite. I detested the idea of Germany being ravaged by war, but I also hoped it meant that Hitler's armies would be defeated, and we'd be safe, that all Jewish people would once again be free in Germany. Instead, Hitler's armies had used the strategy of *blitzkrieg*, an intense campaign of military aggression, for a swift triumph. Before Britain and France could come to Poland's aid, Hitler's forces claimed victory with relentless armored attacks and air assaults on Polish territories.

"That's awful," responded Ben. "The bloodshed is spreading. What will it take to stop that madman?"

"You've no idea how bad it is," sighed Max. Having been upgraded in his security clearance status, he was privy to highly confidential material. "Poland isn't just a territorial success for Hitler," he explained, "it's another way to segregate and exterminate Jews."

Jolting back, I hit my elbow on the wall. "Exterminate Jews!"

"Oh, it's pathetic." Max walked to the far wall of the cellar and stood still. The only sounds I heard were the familiar "voices" the house made—noises I had become accustomed to, and even fondly anticipated. Finally, he turned to face Ben and me. "Do you really want me to tell you what is happening? I don't see how this bad news is of any help to you two."

"We want to know," Ben replied as he looked at me.

Rubbing my throbbing elbow, I nodded agreement. "Yes, and," I stopped to wipe tears from my eyes, "Shana's out there somewhere. Perhaps we'll learn something that might help find her."

"Rumors are being spread by the SS in Poland against the Jews." Max paused. Again.

Seeing my best friend hurting and shamed by what he was telling us—hesitating, shaking his head, and his bleak, downcast countenance—I felt sick to my stomach. "Just say..." I swallowed back food particles that regurgitated into my mouth. "Please Max, just say what you're holding back. It can't be that bad."

"Trust me, it's worse than anything you could imagine." He went on to tell us that the rumors were propaganda to turn the Polish people against the Jews.

"Like what?" asked Ben.

"That Jews carry infectious disease, particularly typhus. That's why they need to be segregated. Jewish neighborhoods are being converted into prisons. To make it easier to identify a Jew, any Jew eleven years or older has to wear a Star of David armband."

When Max stopped talking and we thought that was all he wanted to tell us, Ben said, "It's complete madness."

"That's not the last of it. There's another phase that's worse." I held my breath as Max told us that, once the Jewish neighborhoods had been transformed, Jews would be shipped out to concentration camps. "Experiments will be conducted in these camps."

"What...what kind of experiments?" I asked.

Max swallowed hard. "There's a doctor named Sigmund Rascher, who's designed dangerous human experiments involving high altitudes, freezing and blood coagulation."

"Huh?" I was confused.

"Humans…Jews…are going to be used to test things that, up until now, have been deemed too dangerous to apply to people. Jews will be human guinea pigs—their lives are not as important as scientific discovery. I don't know what the specific programs will entail. I only saw the memo that mentioned planning for this is underway." He released a heavy sigh and raked his fingers through his blonde hair.

I was about to protest this latest Nazi cruelty when Max put up a hand, palm facing out, in a signal I knew meant, *stop.* He said, "That's not all." Max's hands shook as he straightened his collar. I wanted to pick at my skin. I needed to. When my nerves were too much for me to handle, I resorted to the self-destructive habit of picking, scratching, or pinching my skin. At first, the physical pain distracted me from my emotional distress. Then, the act itself became soothing, calming. Ben didn't understand or appreciate my habit, so I stopped for his sake. But as Max revealed layer upon layer of devastating news about the world in which he lived and Shana was lost, I had an overwhelming urge to pluck at myself—to relieve the tension.

"What else, Max?" asked Ben.

"Gas." Max's body shivered. "There are experiments underway using gas to murder people. Initially, they used carbon monoxide to kill the politically undesirable—the disabled. Now, there's talk of exhaust gas and something called Zyklon B, a cyanide compound."

"For use on the Jews?" I shuddered.

Ben, mouth agape, stared at Max.

"Yes." Visibly upset, he broke eye contact with us as he told us the final piece of Hitler's plan. "Buildings with chambers are being planned to gas massive numbers of Jews. What Hitler ultimately has in mind is the total annihilation of all Jewish people."

Max stood motionless.

Ben started to cry.

I slumped to the floor and, ever so weakly, scratched my neck.

Chapter Eighteen

It had been six days since Max last visited us. I was a tightly bound bundle of nerves. I paced and cried in the stark vault we had been living in for way too long: fourteen months.

I was being held a physical prisoner for my safekeeping because of Hitler's war on Jews, and I hated it. Also at the mercy of my imagination, thoughts, memories with no one but Ben to talk to, I developed a tension headache. It had been building for days. My scalp felt like it was being pulled off my head. No amount of rubbing my temples helped.

Clinging to my lifebelt, Ben, I demanded attention. I needed to get my mind off my heartache and obsessive conjecturing about Shana. I needed a breather. The constant rumination of the unthinkable was making me ill. "Ben," I moaned. "Could you please give me a massage? I can't get rid of this headache." When I reached for his arm, he jerked it away from me. And when he turned his back to me, a sharp pain struck my chest "Ben…"

"Leave me alone!" he mumbled.

Ben's rebuff hurt my feelings. I knew he was grieving, the same as I was, but I took it personally. When I reached for his shoulder to turn him around, he resisted. My whispered plea in his ear, "Can I have a hug?" was met with silence. When he refused to embrace me, I exploded and took my agitation out on my punching bag of balled-up dirty laundry. Pounding it over and over until I was longer capable of suppressing my voice, I let him have it. "Stop rejecting me! I can't take it!"

His body jerked backward. "Why you selfish little brat. Everything is about you. You want this. You need that. I have needs as well, and I need to be left alone! And for God's sake, keep your voice down!"

When he turned his back on me again, the damn burst and out came a flood of grief, the linchpin of my anger. A tidal wave of loss, sorrow, disbelief, shock—turbulent emotions all stirred up together—surged out of me. Once the tsunami calmed, I heard Ben laugh. It was as if I cried for both of us. His laughter made me giggle. That day, the laughter and the crying created a pathway to something new.

After that exchange, our relationship changed. Something new had formed. Not quite brother and sister anymore. Something deeper, something different. Ben's rejection had scared me. I realized that, for the first time in my life, I feared being alone. I feared facing each day without a living soul who cared if I lived or died. Ben's turning away from me that day ignited a longing deep in my soul: to have a normal life, with a boyfriend, with intimacy in every way. I needed to be a part of something. To belong to someone. And to have someone belong to me. I realized that everything I desired was reflected in my muddled relationship with my brother. His touch had become a soothing comfort. His attention fed my hunger to be treated like a valuable person. A smile from Ben warmed me more than any number of coats or blankets could. Being able to tend to his needs filled me with a sense of meaning, of indescribable joy. And his rejection triggered my greatest fear: living an empty, vapid life alone. I needed external validation to feel loved, to feel worthy, to feel I was someone. With Max's visits infrequent and brief, Ben was all I had.

Ben and I spent hours talking and opening up about things we didn't want to face: what was happening in Germany, the death of our parents and Lawrence, the mystery of Shana's whereabouts and what she could be going through, and what our futures might be if we made it out of that basement alive. We cried together. We laughed together. And I did get that massage from him. His touch was soothing. And stirring. Tempting. But we never crossed that sexual line. Not that I didn't think about it. But the guilt of what the consequences could have been and how it might have changed our relationship was a chance I didn't want to take.

Besides talking and providing each other solace, we found activities to occupy our attention. We made up games, I continued to draw, we took turns spying through the hole in the wall, and, finally, Ben consented to let me read from one of my books.

He told me he wasn't interested in "that stupid love story," referring to *The Great Gatsby*. I got defensive over him disparaging my affinity for romance. "It's a good story," I whined.

"Oh, come on," he smirked. "Which book do you want to pester me with?" He patted my hand.

I savored the sweet softness of his hand on mine. The warmth in my heart dissolved the walls my ego was building because he criticized one of my favorite books. "*Babbitt*. How about that one? The author, Sinclair Lewis, won the 1930 Nobel Prize in Literature. It's one of my favorites."

"Okay, okay, already." He smiled.

I read while he listened quietly. I wondered if he was even paying attention. Then, he announced that the Babbitt character was an idiot who judged his self-worth by the fact that he owns an alarm clock. "What he owns and how much he owns gives him status. Ridiculous!" And when I commented back about how Babbitt changed and evolved while being on a vacation, Ben said, "You're an incurable romantic. He has a moment in nature, but then look what happens to him and his friend. One lands in jail and the other ends up having an affair. People are people."

Confused by his last statement, I shook my head.

Ben continued, "I just wonder if people ever change? Once corrupt, always corrupt. That's where we differ, Helen. You look at someone and see the sun rising, bringing in the light."

"And you?"

"I see the sun, but I also see it setting. When the afterglow is gone, there's nothing but the dark."

"What's all that supposed to mean?" I shook my head again. "How about speaking a common language?"

"Metaphor, my sis, the sun removes the dark, but it also brings it back when it sets; it's part of the same movement. No one is without a dark side. We're all mixed bags. We'd like to think we're loftier than the next, but we're all shades of the same stuff. Who knows what we'd do given different circumstances? Even Hitler may have—"

"Don't put me in any categories with that monster!"

"There by the grace of God, Helen…" He motioned to my dirty laundry punching bag. "What is it inside of you that pounds that bundle of clothes over there?"

"I'd never kill hundreds of innocent people!" I slammed the book shut.

"For the sake of argument, I agree with you. I believe you don't have a mean bone in your body." He held my arm to still me from further eruptions. "But…"

"I knew there'd be a but." I exhaled. This time, his touch wasn't so endearing.

"Really, we've never been in a position to find out, and I hope to God we never are. I don't know what lives inside of me. Sure, I'd like to believe I'm decent. I want people to like me. I want to feel I do some good in the world and that I'm a good person. But I don't know how good I'd be with a gun pointed at my head."

I had to admit that he made sense. My gut reaction had been a biased self-protective one—that I'd never be able to kill another human being. But when I carefully considered Ben's argument, I knew without a doubt that, given the opportunity to bring my parents and Lawrence back, I'd kill. The same was true for the rest of my family. Then I thought about Max. What would I be willing to do for a friend, for someone not my family? I was sure it wouldn't be pleasant, but I would have to protect them any way I could. It was then I became aware I was capable of committing murder. "I see your point." Making eye contact with Ben, I said, "I hate to admit it, but I think you're right."

Laughing, he said, "Good. I promise not to rub it in."

Our time continued like that, reading the books, arguing back and forth, commiserating over our mutual losses, and trying to get that darn radio to work while fighting back the urge to smash it against a wall.

The peephole brought the outside world in: the animals, plants, clouds in the sky, crisp smells after the rain, and the noises that we never used to pay attention to. Now, it was the noise outside that concerned us the most. The sound of tires approaching. Those were the times Ben and I clung to each other like life rafts.

Chapter Nineteen

After I'd read my books several times, and tidied up the basement as best I could, I cozied up to that little hole in the wall to survey the natural world that had become so foreign to me. I had been in the cellar so long that I could barely remember the feeling of sunshine heating my face or a warm breeze tousling my hair. Although my view was limited, I found a hubbub of activity to keep me entertained. I counted leaves on tree branches, a challenge on a calm day. Noticing that most woodland creatures appeared to be aware that they are being watched, I noted how many minutes between the time an animal scurried around typically, and then stopped—its eyes darting around and its nose twitching, trying to detect danger. These little creatures were not unlike Ben and me when we heard Max approaching. I wondered if those critters had acid bellies, like us, when their muscles remained rigid and motionless. Once, in my life before the cellar, I saw an opossum playing dead. It was at a neighbor's house. Their big black dog found the cataleptic animal in a shrub in their side yard. After sniffing the opossum (which never moved), the dog got down on its haunches with the opossum between its front legs. Wagging its tail, it barked until the owner came out and shooed the dog away. Our neighbor then shoveled up the opossum to throw it in the garbage. That's when the animal got up and ran off. *It sure looked dead,* I thought to myself. Contemplating a threatening situation, I wondered if I could play dead as convincingly.

Standing by the cellar wall waiting for another animal or bird to move into view, I inhaled a whiff of fresh air that came through the small hole. The clean smell of a gentle breeze triggered memories from a happier time—a time when life was normal and I had a family. Lying on the grass in the park when we were on a picnic. Playing ball outside with my siblings. Running around the house in a raucous round of hide-and-seek. I had the advantage of being the smallest and thinnest member of my family, allowing me to fit under beds and snuggle behind long coats in the closets. Just for a moment, I was transported back to my home. I was hiding in my wardrobe, the smell of shoe leather at my feet and wool from my clothes making my nose itch. Back then, I resented having to share a closet with Shana. Not anymore. I missed my dresses arranged by color and hung in order according to how much I liked them. One pair of shoes and one pair of boots always placed side by side neatly. We didn't have many clothes. Our parents felt that we only needed enough to get us through the season. Younger children wore what older children no longer fit into, and I only got a new dress when my old dresses were worn-out. Although they could have afforded more with my father's salary before he was fired for being a Jew, he, in particular, didn't want us spoiled. I think that's partially why I was able to make due with so little to wear in that cellar. I didn't mind doing the washing, and I liked pressing my hands over material on a flat surface as a substitute for ironing. Any task to keep me busy was a distraction from the reality of my situation. And any distraction helped to keep me from going crazy.

Thinking back to my room and life before the cellar, I envisioned the books that my parents had bought me for birthdays and holidays. I saw their titles lining my bookshelf, and smiled. No one would ever extinguish my love of reading. The Hebrew Bible, specifically the Book of Proverbs, jumped out at me while I was mentally scanning my book collection. The German word,

Schadenfreude, which means the enjoyment derived from another's misery, always struck me as odd. Until now. Proverbs warns against *Schadenfreude*, rejoicing in the fallen enemy. I believed we shouldn't even need a rule about this in our Bible; it's common decency. Yet this word of God was lost in Hitler's Germany. Who are these Germans? What kind of people gain pleasure from another's misfortune?

My nervous habit of picking at my body continued despite Ben's disapproval. I also began plucking at my clothing. One of my nails hooked onto a piece of thread on the coat I was wearing. When I pulled at it, a patch of wool just under my left breast puckered. I wished I had my sewing machine to fix it. As I worked the material loose, with my fingers, I felt my left nipple harden. A warm surge of arousal rippled down to my groin. I was amazed that my body could get sensually stimulated in a cold, damp cellar while I constantly feared the present and the future. But I was twenty-one-years-old, and certain parts of my body didn't seem to care that Hitler had ruined my love life.

The cellar was large, but not big enough for the kind of privacy two young people in the prime of their sexual lives needed. Ben also had his desires that he needed to handle.

186

On occasions when he thought I was fast asleep, I heard him masturbating. I covered my mouth so he wouldn't hear me laugh when he tried to make his orgasmic moans sound as if he was snoring. During the few times I was able to reach a peak, I had the same problem; although I pretended to cough. Those were the good times—when the laughter, snores, or sighs would come with the release of pent-up sexual appetites. There were other times when I tried to pleasure myself, and it ended in frustration. Wallowing in self-pity, I worried that I would die without ever being with a man and knowing the pleasure of passionate lovemaking. I dreamed that I would live long enough to regain my freedom, find a man to love me, marry him, and have many children. I wanted what my parents had.

As we were well into our second year, I tried my best to conjure up happier times in the mirror of my mind. Using only the cellar as my whole world, I paid attention to every detail. My senses became acute to the smallest sound, smell, flicker of light, or change in temperature. I took nothing for granted and wasted nothing. Smells gained texture, like the can of soup I left open for too long. What once offered a pleasant, savory aroma reeked of a pungent, nose-pinching insult. I held my nose while choking it down, but I ate it.

Ben smirked. "Good thing you're not wasting any food."

"Oh, be quiet." I gagged, covering my mouth with my hand. When I recovered, I nodded and said, "You're right." Then I handed the can of rancid soup to him.

I spent time focusing on what different parts of my body could offer to help me feel better. My eyes were my allies. I relished how colors changed from something seemingly old and familiar into a delightful kaleidoscope. All I had to do was look with fresh, optimistic eyes, not ones clouded by fear or misery. I was fascinated by the way light transformed a log from brown to dark gray to mossy green, depending on how the light rested. It was down in that cellar that I gained an understanding for, and an appreciation of, how an artist could take an empty canvas and bring it alive with color and shapes.

I used this new way of viewing the world, the cave we were in, to share stories with Ben. I'd start the story and turn it over to him. He usually turned the tale into something silly or pedantic. That's when we would argue. But then we'd laugh at how ridiculous it was to fight over storytelling. We tasted the human condition—how we struggle to survive in difficult and trying circumstances. The pain and hurt remained locked inside, but Ben and I seemed to have found a way to cope with our new life…whatever this new life was.

I heard rain falling outside. The *tap, tap, tap* of the raindrops made me think about life before the cellar—life when I was free, happy, and only worried about silly things. Giggling, I reminded Ben of an afterschool walk home in the rain.

Ben responded to my laughter with, "What?"

"Oh," my laughter increased. "You don't remember?" I went into coughing spasms.

Nonplussed, Ben slapped me on the back. "Helen, get a hold of yourself."

I doubled over in glee and simply couldn't say what I thought was so funny. I'm sure Ben figured I was having a nervous breakdown. I looked and sounded like a lunatic. Trying to keep my noise level at a safe decibel only made me continue to laugh even harder. Finally, I spat out, "I'm fine."

The hilarity got to him, and Ben started to laugh. When I looked at him to speak, the little composure I had managed to muster dissolved into fits of laughter. My ribs and cheeks were sore from all the carrying on. Finally, when my bladder protested and leaked urine into my panties, I heaved a big sigh and stopped the hysteria.

"What was that about?" asked Ben.

"Wait." I went to change my wet undies. I cleaned myself at the sink, washed my garment, changed into something clean and went back to my brother. "Do you remember the day we walked home from school in the rain?"

"Which of the ten million times?" He smirked.

"The day you threw me in a mud puddle!"

"Oh, that day."

"Mamma didn't want to let me in the house." Remembering when I came home caked in mud from head to toe, I started to laugh again. My mother's eyes were daggers. Once showered and back downstairs, I apologized to her. She forgave me. I loved the way she so easily let go of upsets. Smiling, I realized that I was now able to breathe easier when thinking about Mamma. The mirth between Ben and me was rejuvenating. Were we finally healing?

I was grateful for whatever enabled us to laugh that day. Ben and I were alive and surviving surprisingly well while those we loved were dead...or worse. If the guilt I had felt in the face of all that had happened wasn't gone, at least it had lessened. How was that possible? I could barely understand myself, let alone the mysteries of human experience in this vast universe. The more I tried to make sense of something the more I'd see the faultiness in my thinking. I wanted to believe I was intelligent and capable of sorting things out, but, in honesty—in the darkness of the cave I was living in—I discovered that, aside from a few practicalities I had learned, there was so little I could say was "truth."

Feeling humbled, I hoped that the future wouldn't be overwhelmingly painful. I prayed that my life would unfold in a way I could deal with. If I couldn't embrace what awaited me, I hoped I would be able to tolerate it. My father told me, "God gives us only what we can handle." I hoped he knew that as truth.

The Seven Year Dress

Chapter Twenty

After the episode of laughter passed, Ben and I continued to grow closer. We talked more and our conversations were more personal. During wistful moments, we would share our dreams for the future. We would debate "the best" strategy to stop Hitler. Sometimes, we would simply discuss lessons we remembered from school. Conjuring up visual images, I thought of a lesson about a hummingbird, evoking all kinds of visions and sounds in my imagination.

"I wish I could see one of them in person," I said, referring to a hummingbird. The only time I'd seen one was during a classroom film. Ben had seen the same tutorial. Those tiny little creatures were adorned with the most vibrant, beautiful colors. I could hear the thrumming sound they made with their wings beating impossibly fast. The space between my ears became a gramophone, making a low, steady *thrum*. As I listened in my head to the sound of a hummingbird, I moved my feet and hands in a dancing motion. "Oh, how I'd love to see one," I repeated. "They look like little fairy angels."

Ben nodded agreement. "They are amazing little birds." My brilliant brother, who liked to use big words, interjected one of his infamous esoteric comments. "They're dimorphic."

"You had to go and spoil the mood, didn't you?" I joked. "You know what I'm going to say next, so why don't you just tell me?"

"Thought you'd never ask," he smiled. "I read somewhere that, in small-scale species, the males are smaller than the females. In normal-sized species, the males are larger. In lay terms, it's called sexual size."

I whacked his arm. "Oh, you!"

The hummingbird brought rhythm into my bones all day. As I remembered the conversation with Ben about "sexual size" that night, my sexuality stirred. Touching my fleshy parts and becoming aroused had become enjoyable. I relaxed on my blankets feeling contented that I had been able to satisfy my carnal urge for pleasure. And feeling liberated, unencumbered by social convention and having to negotiate with a man—I was able to make my release happen. For a brief few moments, I flew free.

Although never far from my mind or heart, the pain, depression, and anger over the loss of my family lessened as time passed. Maybe I had matured and learned to cope with life's disappointments better. Perhaps time had helped with the healing process. I cultivated the *thrumming* sound of the hummingbird into a psalm. Over and over it played in my head until it morphed into Papa's voice. *Life, above all else, is what is important.* And in communion with my father, I whispered back, *yes Papa,* as I wiped the tears flowing from my eyes.

I pray I make it out of Hitler's hell alive. In the fiery pit Germany had become, I learned a valuable lesson. I couldn't change what life throws at me, but I could determine how I receive it. Positive thinking felt good. Negative thoughts were painful. If I could do anything to help myself for the rest of my life, it would be to monitor my thoughts. And not let my worries drag me down into a dark grave of my creation. Ben said to me a while ago, "You choose sunlight." *I must remember his words.* I couldn't help wondering, however, would my new philosophy be strong enough if the nightmare turned deadly vicious?

Stubborn and persistently curious about the forbidden "upstairs," I moved toward the steps. Boredom had consumed me. I ached for something new. I desperately wanted out of that cellar. I longed to find a large window to gaze through, to see more of the world than that tiny hole allowed. *If I could just open an outside door and breath in more than a few ounces of fresh air and feel a breeze upon my cheeks...* I looked up at the door at the top of the stairs. Placing a foot on the first step, I said, "I think it's safe for us to go up there." With my attention on Ben, I moved up two more steps. "This is an isolated farm, kilometers from anyone seeing us." I advanced another step. "I want to see sunlight come through a window. Come with me."

"No!" he snapped. "Don't do it!"

"But Ben, it—"

"Don't 'but Ben' me. It's too dangerous. Get back down here and go look through your peephole if you need a dose of sunlight."

"Ben," I whined, advancing up another step.

Jumping up and rushing to me, he tripped over the edge of a blanket and crashed down on his knees. Writhing in pain, he cradled his legs up to his chest. His agony didn't stop him from bossing me around. "Get down here, now!

You're a spoiled brat, Helen Stein! You'll get us both killed."

"Oh no! Ben...are..."

"Ouch!" He pressed his leg.

Feeling a jumble of emotions, I rushed back to him. I was fearful that he might have fractured a limb. But I was also frustrated that, in a society of two, I had no control. Ultimately, and because I caused him harm with my selfishness, guilt won out, "I'm sorry. I'm sorry. Oh, please don't be hurt."

"I am hurt!" He stretched out his legs, moving them gingerly, to assess the extent of his injuries. When he decided his legs weren't broken, he undid his pants to look at the damage. "Scrapes. This time. I'm lucky. But you...I could hit you, Helen! This isn't some game we're playing. Our parents were murdered! So was Lawrence and God knows where Shana is, if she's even alive. You want to kill us too?"

He made his point. Feeling awful, I burst into tears. "I don't want to think about that! I don't need to be reminded of what happened. I know what happened! But sometimes I feel like I'm going to go insane if I don't get out of this place. Ben, please understand..."

"You don't think I feel the same way? I do. Oh my God, I do." He pulled me to him and held me. I don't know where my crying ended and his started in that dance of pain. Would remembering always have such sharp edges? When his breathing calmed and the angry redness left his face, he wiped tears from mine. "You're all I have left," he said.

Every thought, every reaction I'd had in the last several minutes, disappeared into an intense trembling. My body felt like I was grabbed by the shoulders and literally shaken to bring me back to my senses. My heart, beating out of control, sent a wave of heat coursing through my body. I felt as if I was heating the damp air around me with the warmth radiating off my body.

Ben's words, "You're a spoiled brat!" ricocheted in my brain. He was right. I was being selfish. Ben and I had the same fear: losing each other. We also had the same motives for harping on each other. Love. Preservation of the only family we knew we had left.

I found my voice and spoke softly, the warmth still radiating from my body. "You've been a pain because you love me. You don't want me to die." I tenderly brushed back a few locks of his hair that had fallen over his moist, gentle eyes. "I love you too, Ben. With all my heart." We hugged for a long time. Our embrace was sweet and tender and filled me with a satisfaction that no amount of fresh air could have provided. I was breathing in my brother's love.

That moment moved us to confess our innermost thoughts and worries—those dreadful, private ruminations that kept us awake at night and that we hadn't dared speak aloud. Our own deaths. My fanciful thinking about feeling a breeze of air upon my cheek dissipating into the harsh reality that my entire family and extended family may all be dead, annihilated because of Hitler's Final Solution to the Jewish Question! How quickly an innocent gesture or word could set off an ugly domino effect ending in misery, whether in the cellar or outside. Exterminating Jews and others as if they were vermin.

Conversations with my brother melded with what Max had alluded to in the memos he'd seen, but they hadn't gelled into a stark reality until Ben's words, "We could be killed with the rest of Jewish population," shot into me. Ben and I talked about Hitler's plan, the one Max said was going to be implemented. Not sure if that would ever impact Ben and me, undulating nausea waved through me as I recalled Max's description of the global plan to exterminate all Jews. Genocide. I worried that Ben and I would be put to death like dirty bugs. We were not guilty of any crime or any misdemeanor. We had not spoken out against them with slanderous or libelous speech. What had we done, besides being born Jewish, to deserve such a fate? Like an overpopulated kennel for dogs, we would be euthanized if we were caught. The disgust in my body tightened into knotted muscles, and my stomach seized into fits of vomiting. My lunch of soup came up. When there was nothing left, green bile spewed from my gut. I grabbed myself to stop the relentless spasms gripping my belly to no avail. I couldn't release the images in my head of human beings being killed by gas. Hordes of them!

I told Ben about that long-ago night when the SS killed Mr. Fineburg. "He was down on his knees with his hands behind his head. A single shot and he fell to his sidewalk grave. His poor family was forced to watch. All because he asked, *why?* Our darling brother, Lawrence, asked the same question. He, too, was murdered. That goddamn question also cost the lives of my father and my mother! For what? For what?" My stomach lurched again.

Ben rubbed my back. He remained silent.

When nothing more came up from my gut, I went into spasms of dry heaving. Then, I noticed that Ben left my side.

He returned to me with a cold rag for my face. "Here. Take this. It should help. I hope." With another rag, he cleaned the mess of vomit from the floor.

"Ben," I sobbed, "do you think they're all gone?"

"Who?" he asked.

"Uncle Abe and Aunt Minnie, cousins Yesh, Roz, Sarah, Yael, Sadie…" I listed our extended family. "Papa's and Mamma's parents—our grandparents." They had visited us for every important occasion, coming by train across Germany until Hitler seized power. All visiting stopped. "They were gentle, kind people. I don't want to think about what may have happened to them." A shiver ran through my body.

Ben looked at me for a moment, his lips parting as if he was about to answer me. Then he sighed, turned away, and continued to mop up the mess I had made.

Neither of us slept well that night. The next day, I couldn't muster any sunshine clichés. Ben didn't have any cheerful metaphors. All we did was cry and mope around. Our doldrums lasted until a pounding blizzard hit the farm.

Thunder and lighting roared until the snowstorm turned into rain and hail hammering the roof. We thought we were being attacked.

Max didn't arrive for his regular visit, leaving us short on supplies and news. He probably had to postpone travel until the weather cleared. By the time he finally came, he found Ben and me huddled together, trying to stay warm next to a small fire. The storm outside had passed; the one that had raged inside of us had also calmed. But it was only a temporary lull before a more ferocious tempest would rip my world to smithereens.

Chapter Twenty-One

In the winter of our fourth year of hiding, another stormy night with rumbling, menacing thunder kept me awake. It began subtly—a faint, low, distant growl. As it grew closer and the grumbling intensified, I knew a mighty tempest was on the horizon. I had to see the magnitude of the storm, so I got up and squinted through the peephole. I used to love storms, especially the pounding sound of rain lashing my bedroom window. And the exhilaration I felt when it was over, breathing in fresh, clean air. But this storm scared me. I saw flashes of lightning in the distant sky as the heavens broke open with a drum roll. *Crack! Bang!* The farmhouse shook. I jumped back from the wall. Another wave of rumbling rolled overhead. A violent, explosion boomed. My body shook with the winter's salvo. It reminded me of loud gunshots. Between claps of the ominous thunder bullying the countryside, I heard another—more troubling—noise. Tires on gravel. I froze. My body tingled as if being stung by a swarm of bees. I could smell the acrid scent of my fear. Max wouldn't come out in this weather. He'd specifically told us that he would stay away in dangerous conditions.

Rain dripped over the hole blurring the view outside. I tried to poke something through to clear it; it was useless. If Max's car was out there—if anyone's vehicle was out there—I couldn't see it. Maybe I hadn't heard tires driving on the gravel road leading to the farmhouse. The last few nights had been fitful for both Ben and me, and I didn't want to wake him now that he'd finally fallen asleep. Like the pouring water outside, my underarms dripped with sweat. I shivered from the cold and anxiety. Still straining to see a vehicle through the small peephole, I wiped my forehead to remove the perspiration threatening to sting my eyes. Nothing. Minutes passed. No one entered the farmhouse. I didn't hear another noise resembling tires driving up to our hiding place. Even though the storm continued to rage, I breathed easier.

Three hours later, Max arrived. Pacing agitatedly, in rapid-fire talk, he said, "I think I was followed. I'm not sure if I lost them." He put down the groceries and a suitcase he had with him.

Ben, now awake, asked, "Them?"

"I thought the SS was on my tail," Max's saucer-like eyes darted around frantically. He shook his head, stopped his frenetic movement, looked to Ben, and then me. "It wouldn't be good for you."

"You lost them. We'll be okay." I put my hand on his arm. "You have a farm out here so why would it be unusual for you to visit it?"

"In the winter? In a storm?" Max continued pacing. "In the middle of the night!"

Ben's voiced cracked and was several pitches too high when he commented on what I'd said. "She's not thinking clearly. She's..." At what looked like a loss for words, he paused to take a deep breath and continued. "She's scared." He ran his hands through his hair, got up, and started pacing along with Max. Ben acted and sounded as frightened as the rest of us.

Ben was right. I was scared. "What now?" I asked.

Max took a slow, deep breath. "We wait and stay calm." He held his arms out to us. "Come here." Hugging them, I felt the trembling tension ease from our bodies.

Max went to a bag he'd brought. "Something for you, Helen."

When he handed a dress to me, I started to cry. He knew I loved my dresses, how they made me feel appealing, special. Boys paid attention to me when I had a nice dress on. This dress was a symbol of normalcy, my femininity, and my past. And I prayed it would also be my future. I hoped to see a day when I would be free to be out in the streets enjoying my life in a lovely new dress.

The two dresses I'd been wearing in the cellar were filthy. Scrubbing the cellar's grime from them with soap at the sink couldn't remove the stains that had become part of the threadbare fabric. Grease and years of dirt covered everything in the cellar. Safety was worth the sacrifice in cleanliness—Ben and I had agreed. But both my dear brother and best friend understood how much I missed feeling like a proper young woman, and how much a new dress means to a proper young woman.

"Don't cry." Ben's smooth, honey-like voice flowed to my ears, making me weep all the harder.

The fear I felt about my uncertain future during that night when the heavens erupted was momentarily eased by Max's simple act of kindness. "Oh Max, you remembered," I said, referring to the many times I spoke to him about how I adored my dresses, about fabric, style, and how wearing a pretty dress made me feel alive. "This one is so beautiful. I'm going to save it for my first day out of here."

A furrowed-brow straightened on Ben's worried face. "Try it on." I could hear the happiness in his voice.

With a smile starting somewhere deep inside me and radiating out to every corner of the cellar, I nodded. Skipping to a place behind the woodpile, I shrugged off my coat and the dirty dress I'd worn for two weeks. I slipped into my new, clean, beautiful dress: a blue cotton floral print with swirls of designs surrounding flowers. My fingers moved over the fabric, encircling the rose petals and luscious green leaves on the pattern. For a brief moment, it wasn't a dress, but nature—and I was encircled in it. Soft and flowing, it was a little loose from the weight I'd lost being in the cellar. But it fit comfortably, and I loved Max for doing this wonderful thing that made me feel beautiful. And hopeful.

As a fashion model on a runway, I emerged from behind my "curtain" of stacked wood and sashayed around Ben and Max, making sure they saw every angle of me in my new dress. "It's the most perfect dress I've ever owned." Hugging Max, I said, "Thank you, my friend. I love you!" Out of the corner of my eye, I saw Ben furtively wiping away tears.

Suddenly, a very piercing howl of wind and throaty growl of thunder ended our gaiety. It was deafening like an airplane flying within feet of us. Unsure and unsettled, I looked to the ceiling, "Thunder?" I squeaked.

"Yes," smiled Max. "It sounds like a big, fancy passenger train whisking lovers away on honeymoons."

Ben winked at Max and played along to lighten my anxiety. "No," he smiled, "It's a lion."

Ben and Max laughed. So did I. "Oh, you two. Well, if it's only a man-eating lion or a speeding train heading for us, then we have nothing to fear. Thanks, I feel so much better!"

"There. See? No one's come. We're safe," said Ben.

Running my hand over the gentle folds on the waistline of my new dress, I felt the soft texture of the cotton. "I hope so."

After a while of light banter to pass the time, Ben's smile faded. "What's the latest on the devil's plan?"

As always, Max hesitated by asking us, "Are you sure you want me to tell you these things after the fright we just had with the thunder? What good can come from you knowing a mouthful of horrible information?"

Max had a good point. I hated hearing about Hitler's plans and atrocities but knowing might make both Ben and me better prepared for whatever might happen. Having lost control over our freedom, knowledge was power; it was all we had left to help ourselves if we were discovered.

I nodded. "I want to know. How else can we prepare for what's next?"

"I agree. It's always better to know," said Ben.

Max sighed. "All right." He spoke of one of the camps, Auschwitz—a network of concentration camps in Polish areas annexed by Germany. They were the main camps doing the gas experiments. When prisoners arrived there, they were assigned a camp serial number.

"Like the Star of David armbands that you told us about?" I naively asked.

"No." Max's voice lowered with regret when he continued. "These are tattoos."

Startled, I jerked back. "On their bodies? Like branding cattle?"

"I'm afraid so," Max replied.

"For everyone who is admitted there?" Ben leaned in closer to Max.

"Only the prisoners selected for work."

"Oh, so not everyone is branded. Some are…" I oozed disgusted sarcasm, "…untainted? I suppose it wouldn't be a Jew who was exempt."

A gray pallor stained Max's complexion. He averted his eyes from mine to the floor. When he opened his mouth to speak, he took a few seconds to respond. "The ones who aren't marked are sent directly to the gas chambers to die."

Blood drained from my brain, and I felt faint. I lost my balance. Max looked up in time to catch my wobbling body before I fell. "Animals!" I yelled. "Who treats human beings like that? What is in the place where their hearts should be!" I heard myself screeching.

Max was still holding my shoulders when he asked, "You okay? You're turning white, Helen."

I took my time to regain my footing. "It's so violent, disgusting, and… I don't have the words." I went silent, into a dark place where the seeds of depression grow. The bleak impermanence of everything I knew, held close, and loved was like a gossamer fabric that was falling apart and taking me with it. Faces of my family members ran through my head like a slow-moving motion picture. I saw them trudging in a funeral march into a room, the room of death. Painfully frightened, they stood not knowing their fate as each breath robbed them of oxygen. And once it dawned on them what was happening, a horrible panic ensued. Screaming. Wailing. Praying. People clinging to each other. People pushing and shoving. Mothers crushing their infants to their chests. Bloody hands from clawing at doors that would never open into freedom. Poor people. Sick people. Jewish people. My family's last moments on earth. *If life is a precious gift (as Papa believed with all of his heart), where is the blessing in living only to die in this unimaginably cruel way?*

Lost in this heinous vision, I became disoriented, but only briefly. Relief washed over me when I realized that I was in the cellar, and Ben and Max were standing by me. They looked concerned. "You're dripping wet," my brother said.

Then, as if pulled under water by a vicious sea monster, the image of my sister engulfed me. Submerged in the delusion, I lost contact with my senses again. I saw her beautiful eyes shining like they always did when she was young and lighthearted. Those beautiful brown eyes

211

morphed into shadowy holes surrounded by black circles. They cried out for help. *Spare me!* She disappeared into the mass of bodies begging for mercy. Spewing poisonous fumes, the airtight gas chamber was an impassive, efficient executioner. The hallucination faded as the last voice cried out, *God save us!* "Shana," I moaned. At that moment, I knew that if I wasn't captured and killed, that I'd go insane. My new dress was sticking to my quaking body.

"You need to get out of that dress." Ben motioned to help me remove it.

"No! Leave me alone." I waved him off and backed away.

"At least put this on." He moved my arms into my coat as the moist material of the dress clung to my body. I wanted to lie down and die. It was all too much. They moved me to my bed and helped lower me onto it. With them beside me, I cried myself to sleep. When I awoke, Max was gone, and Ben was nodding off at my side. Hearing me move, he asked, "Are you all right?"

The sleep had helped and, although I felt as if I was run over by the passenger train Max had joked about, I was fine. "I think so," was all I said.

Later, Ben told me that Max stayed with us longer than he should have. He refused to leave me, knowing how upset I was. "I told him to go and that I'd take care of you. I was worried he'd draw more suspicion to himself."

My stomach knotted. "I hope he's safe."

How could we have foreseen that nothing would keep any of us safe?

Chapter Twenty-Two

I was still in my coat and new dress when the door to the cellar crashed open. Thick leather boots thudded down the stairs. Five rifle-wielding SS surrounded us. Intimidated by their gray uniforms with skull-like insignias on their green collars, I cowered. A chill ran down my spine. Pointed Gewehrs were aimed at our heads when an overweight, tall man blasted down the stairs carrying a huge whip in one hand and a Lugar pistol in the other. He up-motioned his gun at us.

I stumbled to stand, to get my bearings. Ben didn't move. "Up!" barked one of the officers.

Ben fumbled to his feet, but his legs wouldn't hold him. He wobbled before he fell back down.

"Are you deaf, pig?" The goliath, overbearing officer with the whip spat at Ben. "Get up! Now!"

An officer, who looked no older than Ben (twenty-six), shouted something with such venom that I could barely make out what he said. My heart flew into my throat. The pounding in my ears obliterated all sounds but my internal panic. Fear had robbed me of my voice and ability to hear, but I could still see. I saw my brother trembling as he tenuously stood next to me.

The ominous, obese officer swiped the crop across his thigh in a threatening gesture. "Fie! So, we have found another pigsty," he smirked and swaggered toward me. His breath upon my face smelled of peppermint schnapps. "You are little for a swine." He moved the butt end of the whip across my face and down into the opening of my coat. Spreading the lapel, his hand slid lower on the rod, close to my left breast. With his other hand, he put his pistol in the holster on his leather belt. Bringing that hand up more deftly than I imagined such a fat man could, he slapped me across my cheek with such force that he knocked me into Ben. Ben's body tensed against mine. I could tell that my big brother wanted to protect me. Fearing he would lash out and get himself killed, I quietly squeezed his arm and searched his eyes in a silent plea for him to stay calm. "A smart Jew..." The fat officer turned to his subordinates— their weapons pointed—and continued, "She knows not to open that slovenly mouth of hers."

The group of sycophants signaled agreement with their laughs. "Yeah, yeah," came their imbecilic responses.

I wanted to confiscate one of their guns and shoot all of them through their hearts. I wanted warm bullets to find their frigid, calculating, stone-hard souls.

The commander spoke in a low, even tone when he said, "Today is your lucky day. You are being transferred out of this pigsty." His words, and the way he spoke them, sounded hopeful, but this ogre didn't seem capable of anything but malevolence. Then, as if by some dastardly design, he read my mind and replied, "You are going to one of our relocation camps."

The word *camp* sent me into a silent panic. Ben's wide-eyed look made me feel sick to my stomach. I couldn't get enough air to fill my lungs because my breaths were so shallow. When I started to hyperventilate, one of the SS who looked too much like Max grabbed me under my arms and dragged me up the stairs. The front of my legs hit each riser so that they were aching and bloody when he finally released me outside. After a few steps that felt like moving through quicksand, I fell once again. As the younger SS cursed several foul-sounding words under his breath, he yanked my arms and dragged me. My feet dangled behind like a swimmer trying to stay afloat as I desperately tried to stand on them and walk while being manhandled. With snow and dirt stuck to my legs, he threw me in the back of a bread truck the Nazis had converted to haul prisoners.

Ben was marched out of the farmhouse with rifles held to his back. He was able to walk. Barely. Droplets of sweat froze on his forehead when he reached the cold outside air. His bulging eyes were as wide as oceans. I ached at the sight of his terrified defenselessness. They shoved him into the truck and slammed the door. Helping me to my feet, Ben whispered, "Are you all right?"

I looked at him. Our fear comingled. Too afraid to speak, my jaw locked. I grabbed his hand. Tightly. We heard a cacophony of noises outside: shouted commands, chaotic replies, and "yes, commandant," over and over. And crackling sounds. Through a few open spaces on the side of the truck, waves of warm air and smoke seeped in. They had set the farmhouse on fire. Peels of laughter told me that they enjoyed watching our hiding place—our home for four years—burn. The wind was knocked out of me. I felt a sense of grief too deep for tears. For all of this to have happened, Max's fears about being followed must have been real. And if those fears were true, Max was surely dead. *Who would protect us now?*

I heard more rapid-fire commands that I didn't want to understand. Then the doors to the truck popped open. Four of the SS entered. Giving us disgusted looks, they sat on the bench opposite to us. I heard Commander Goliath and another voice in the driver's compartment when the vehicle's engine sputtered and started. We had traveled several kilometers over bumpy terrain before any of them spoke.

"Too bad they aren't still using this to gas the pigs," said the young SS, who earlier had dragged me to the truck. He continued, directing his civil-sounding comments to Ben, "This truck had been used for gassing…you know, extermination, but, now that it's old with cracks and holes on the sides, it's no longer effective for, well, you know." He smiled. "So we use it to gather pigs."

One of the more mature SS, sternly said, "Quiet! Do you want to start a panic when they get to the train?" He turned to Ben and me, and, with a repugnant, serpentine smile, said, "My youthful friend here misspoke. There is some mistake. A rumor. We assure you this relocation is in your best interest."

Best interest! Again, I wanted to grab the rifle out of his hands and impale him with it. I would gladly watch the life flow out of his body and the body of every single Nazi who had tortured and murdered my family, my friends, and my people. An invisible vise-like restraint compressed my body. Something hindered me from taking action. I knew that if I did anything but sit still and silent, it would be the last thing I ever did on this earth. *Stay alive,* my Papa's loving words came through to me. I held on to that. I was alive. Ben was alive. The memories of the warmth from my Papa, my Mamma, and my family were all I had to hold onto. And I held onto them for dear life.

The ride from Brandenburg seemed long; I tried my best not to think about the horrors of the camps Max had shared with us. I forced my mind to focus on what my eyes were seeing and my ears were hearing, and I used my senses to keep each moment as calm as possible. When one of them lit a cigarette with a match, I noticed their shiny boots and the different positions of their feet. The older officer's legs were rigid with no space in between. I assumed he was the second-in-command. I feared him the most. He had an eerie, disingenuous expression when he spoke that unnerved me. A dog we used to have, Greta, popped into my mind. When Greta sensed danger, her hackles stood up. Just like with my dog, the hair on the back of my neck painfully tingled around that officer. My instincts told me what I needed to know. For now, I knew that as long as we kept quiet and remained submissive, we wouldn't be killed. Again, my father's advice came to me, *no sass.* The wisdom of my body melded with the wisdom from my Papa that lived on in me.

After a while, the bumpy road smoothed to what felt like a conventional highway. The noise of driving over forest terrain quieted. I overhead what one of the SS whispered to another. "That idiot had to buy her a dress."

I knew from that comment how we'd been discovered. The thought of Max's selflessness and generosity made my legs feel numb. Someone must have seen him buying it and reported him for doing it. Purchasing a dress when he didn't have a female companion must have roused suspicion. Max's simple act of kindness to lift my spirits brought those demons to our location. And brought an end to his life. There would be no leniency for a traitor to the Führer, especially for one helping Jews. All the years he served their cause would not afford him a reprieve. He had betrayed Hitler. The only saving grace was that Max's personal secret remained safe with me; it never came back to haunt him.

I was saddled with the facts about my dear friend when we arrived at the train station. The commander-in-charge put his face inches from mine. I was forced to smell his acrid breath and feel the slime as he spewed spittle when he said, "Oh yes, I forgot to mention that your friend, Mr. Müller, is dead." Once again, he opened the lapel of my coat. He looked me up and down then grabbed the material covering my breasts. "The Jew lover died for this!" He released his grip on my dress and grabbed my left breast. A cold shudder rippled through me.

Although I sensed that Max was dead, hearing it from this monster, who glowered at me as if I was his next victim, made me weak in the knees. The world became blurry. As the environment spun around me, this hateful, pathetic excuse for a human being commanded, "Hold her up!" SS hands on my arms made my skin crawl. As if this wasn't enough, the repulsive loathsome commander wouldn't simply leave me to my grief and fear. He had to add one parting insult to rape me with his words. "A shame to lose a good Aryan specimen on a filthy Jew shoat." It was the last thing I heard before I passed out.

When I came to, I was on the ground with Ben by my side. The abhorrent SS, who transported us, were gone. As he helped me to my feet, I saw what must have been hundreds of men, women, and children standing at the station. SS used their pointed guns to motion confused, terrified people into already filled cars without windows. I thought of farmers herding cattle; only farmers were more humane with their livestock. The moaning and pleading coming from the opened doors were unbearable. "Please," a hand reached out to the SS standing there, "water." The poor man was slammed back with the butt of a rifle. The nauseating stench of urine and feces greeted Ben and me as the SS shoved us into a crammed compartment that would take us to God knows where.

Chapter Twenty-Three

I had heard from one of the other prisoners who had been on the train a couple of days that the train we were in had low priority. It would proceed to the mainline only after all other transportation was concluded. That meant we remained in the freight car in the layover yard for hours, stalled, in a suffocating, living hell. Many people had already been in there for two to three days on what was supposed to be a four-day journey. Along with the herd of people, some on death's door babbling inaudible pleas for help from their parched mouths, Ben and I huddled together in the middle of the car. We bounced off others as we tried to inch our way to a side wall for support. Ben managed to rest an elbow on one of the sides. His other sweat-drenched arm clung to mine as the train began to move slowly.

Max had mentioned the trains to us, the ones taking prisoners to occupied Poland. He told us that the maximum capacity proposed by the SS regulations was supposed to be no more than 50 per car. I didn't believe that 50 people would fit in a railway car. How could I be so right and so wrong at the same time? These cars couldn't humanely accommodate 50 people; yet there I was packed in with probably at least 70 men, women, and children. The SS gave us nothing: no food or water. The only latrine was a bucket. One bucket. Only those people near to it could use it. The rest of us were crammed in so tightly that we could barely move from side to side, let alone navigate our way to an overflowing container of human waste. Splatters of feces, puddles of urine and sprays of vomit covered the floors and the walls. And when there was no food left to vomit, bile came from the weak and dehydrated. A tiny barred window allowed for inadequate ventilation.

Witnessing the collective terror, panic, and agony was torturous enough to leave scars on my soul that never healed. Worse still was living among the dead and watching the dying. I will never forget the man who gasped for air from lack of oxygen or the woman who froze to death from the elements. How could anyone freeze to death while virtually blanketed with warm, albeit sickly and unfamiliar, bodies? It was just one more Nazi savagery to boggle my already muddled mind. I'm sure many succumbed because they gave up. The weather probably pushed them over the edge. I hated the sounds of wheezing lungs desperately trying to breathe through the overcrowding. We were all suffocating. I panicked when a man pressed into my chest, knocking the air out of me. Were it not for Ben shoving him away, I might have been another body rattling on the floor.

The worst of it was the stench of rotted flesh permeating the car. A mother cried into a bundle in her arms—the five-month-old deceased daughter she couldn't abandon. As people weakened, they moaned for water that never came. Men searched through their pockets for anything that might pry a door open to throw the decaying bodies out and offer freedom to those who dared to jump. They were not successful in releasing anyone from that living coffin.

As the train moved on, insanity beset a few who, like us, had lost everything. Among a couple of the incoherent prisoners was a loud and unruly man who went into an angry, babbling rampage on the man beside him. The victim fell unconscious after hitting his head on the side of the car. He died a day later. After two days of enduring this perdition, I went numb and fell into an abyss. I stared into the dead space below the ceiling of the car or into the other blank eyes that mirrored my soul.

When one kindhearted man suggested we sing, a group of others yelled for him to stay quiet. This moving inferno on wheels was driving us all to madness. How much can the human spirit endure? How much worse could it get?

I would know soon.

The train stopped several days later. I was weak from the exhaustion of standing the entire time while leaning on Ben and trying to keep my thoughts off our destination: a death camp. Due to the cold, the lack of any rest, our unending fright, and the overcrowded, unsanitary conditions on that transport, Ben's bronchitis returned. He didn't have a fever yet, but if he didn't get the proper care, I knew he wasn't strong enough to survive whatever the Nazis had in store for us.

The doors of the car finally opened, blinding us with light even though the day was gloomy. Officers barked orders for us to get out, which was no easy task. We were a feeble, shaky, drained, brittle lot. Our path out of the car wasn't clear, either. We stumbled over corpses in various stages of decay on our way out of the car.

Ben and I were scarcely able to move our feet forward once upon solid ground. Guards used their rifles to push us into different lines. When the lines were formed to their satisfaction, the guards ordered us to march. We stayed in formation, but our pace was sluggish—not the brisk, enthusiastic stride of Nazis on the hunt. We were the hunted. Captured, our bodies were hunched over from agony, fatigue, sorrow and fear. Wanting to be invisible but ever the curious girl, I looked up briefly. Ahead I saw a gate. The gate to hell. Over the entrance were the words *ARBEIT MACHT FREI* (work sets you free). Max had mentioned that this was part of the false public relations campaign—the deceitful way of promoting fictitious hope that hard work would result in our liberation. Would a real work camp offering freedom have needed such a high, perilous barbed-wire fence surrounding it? The disgusting truth was that the internees were damned to slave labor or death. I quickly lowered my heavy, tired head. I knew in my soul I'd do what I needed to stay alive.

I was fairly certain we were in Poland, but I wasn't sure which living cemetery of a camp we were entering. Someone whispered, "Auschwitz." Max's words wrapped around my brain, *the main camps doing the gas experiments, and when prisoners arrived there they were assigned a camp serial number.* I later found out that it was strategically located at the crossroads of many Polish cities; so relocating Jews from German-occupied Europe as well as Germany was quite convenient. The Nazis designed the concentration camp to maximize efficiency in their efforts to transport and exterminate millions of Jews.

Looking at the fearful faces, the grief-stricken mothers holding onto their children, and father's pleading for mercy for their families, I wondered how much these people knew. They didn't have someone like Max, who kept us informed of the atrocities. And because of the geography, in a large isolated area, the news from the death camps would be kept from the outside world. It was the Nazis concerted effort to hide what they were doing. Given the magnitude of these facilities, these sadists would have to locate them in remote areas. Max had said Auschwitz was large—at least 40 square kilometers on the inside and five kilometers surrounding the perimeter. Dear old Max, he was right about everything. I noticed some two-story buildings, which I assumed were for the SS. Other buildings looked like austere brick barracks.

Prisoners moved to where the SS officers divided people. We were still several people back, but we were able to witness a mother clinging to her young child. As they pulled the small boy from her grip, he screamed, "Mamma!" The unthinkable happened when, in hysterics, she ran to her son. They were both shot and dragged away like sacks of potatoes. Tired, weak men and women gasped and cried as children clung to them. One man ran to the SS yelling, "Monsters!" The guards made him an example of what kind of behavior they wouldn't tolerate. He was clubbed until his head burst open and gray substance oozed from his nose. The last few people ahead of us moved to the front of the line. When a father was separated from his teenage daughter, he spat on one of the officers. Both the man and his daughter were shot in the face as the rest of us stood there in shocked disbelief.

Ben's cough turned into dry heaves.

The violent mental and emotional strain was too much for me to process. I shut down as human beings were divided into two lines: the old, the young, and the infirmed in one, and the able-bodied in the other. Feeling numb, I watched as a tall, sinister SS officer pointed a rifle at my brother and said, "You!"

My very weak, dehydrated, ill brother tried to straighten his slumped body to look at the man. "Yes, sir," his voice cracked.

"To the left," he ordered.

Ben's eyes pleaded when his mouth mumbled, "Please sir, may I stay with my sister?"

For asking a simple question, my brother, my beloved Ben, was shot. His blood splattered on my dress. My dress: the reason we ended up in this hellhole. Frozen in shock, I stood silently, shaking, too dehydrated for tears, while my brother's death squad stood laughing and making jokes.

My brother's executioner turned to me. I mouthed, "I sew."

"Speak up!"

I tried to moisten my cracked lips with my parched tongue. I repeated, "I sew clothes."

"To the right," he pointed. I received the tattoo on my left forearm. My life was spared for now. But for what? My father's words no longer held meaning because my life was now unbearable.

Would I live to feel differently?

Chapter Twenty-Four

After being branded, I was stripped naked. A wave of sharp indignation knotted my stomach as my feminine modesty and virtue were robbed from me. I averted my eyes off the horrible sight of women marching naked in front of laughing, jeering SS. With Nazis watching on as if Auschwitz was a brothel, we lined up at the next station in our slaughterhouse. It was where our heads were shaved.

I wanted to grab the razor out of the dispassionate hands that butchered my head—the hands that stole the last of my femininity—and treated me worse than a sheep being sheared. Stroke upon stroke, I listened to that awful buzzing sound. I felt my identity fall away with each pass of the razor. Any objection from me would result in a beating or death, so I stood there and let them obliterate...me. Would there be anything left of me worth saving after this?

Patches of my beautiful, brown, curly hair still clung to my body as I was marched to the shower. I grabbed hold of a lock and held on to the strands tightly as the ice-cold water ran over my body. I wept as the last wisps of my hair washed from my hand and circled the drain.

After the shower, I was given an ugly sack to wear as a dress and wooden shoes. No undergarments. I no longer felt like a woman in the bleak, dull, beige dress I had to put on. It was the first time in my life that I hated a dress—if it could even be called a dress. With its circular slit for my head, flaps for sleeves and piece of material to wrap around my waist, this garment truly was a sack. I despised how that ugly prison uniform looked and what it represented: Nazi criminal indecency and injustice. I wanted to burn that symbol of hatred and persecution. I wanted to grab back the dress Max had given me, but it coexisted somewhere in a pile of prisoners' clothes the Nazis had confiscated.

The next stop was a line where prisoners received water. A scrawny man gave me a half-filled tin cup.

Grabbing it with both hands, I gulped down all of it. Nausea from dehydration forced it back up. I felt a hand on my back. I jumped.

"Sips. Take sips." Her voice was gentle.

I lifted my head and saw a kind, soft face with worn wrinkles and bloodshot eyes. She stood by my side and told the man to please refill my mug. "Try again, but slower, my dear."

This time, it stayed down.

Exhausted and traumatized, I cried, but no tears fell from my dried-out eyes. I tried to mutter, "Thank you." A sigh was all I could manage.

The woman smiled. "I understand," she said. "My name is Ester."

I grabbed her hand, and, with the little energy left in mine, gave it a squeeze. Still holding my hand, she led me to a brick building that looked as if it was constructed hastily and with few resources. There was no insulation, heating, or sanitary facility. A bucket was used for elimination. My feet sunk into the marshy ground as she walked me to a hard, wooden-framed bunk bed. Atop it was a filthy straw mattress stained with urine and feces. My knees buckled. Ester grabbed hold of my arm and steadied me.

"This is better than the other one," she said. "There's another that's a wooden stable-barrack. It used to hold over fifty horses, but now it holds several hundred prisoners. They sleep on wood slabs."

As she was orienting me to what I might expect there, I felt something brush against my leg. A rat began to climb up my calf. I tossed it off with a jerk of my limb. "Oh, God," I moaned.

Ester watched the rodent scurry away. "The dampness from leaky roofs, soiled mattresses, and stench brings these uninvited guests," she said in an apologetic tone.

Standing there shaking my head, trying to bring some reality to this overwhelming situation, I was speechless.

"You'll be close to my bed, and perhaps we'll have work duty together." Ester then warned me about the false friendships of the *kapos*, prisoners with privileges. "Remember that they will betray you for a morsel of moldy bread."

"I work in the kitchen peeling potatoes. It's a good job. Easy compared to other jobs here." Ester continued to tell me that the prisoners received three meals a day: those doing less physical work got 700 calories while those doing heavy labor received slightly more. Breakfast consisted of a hot drink. The remaining meals were composed of watery soup made with potatoes, and occasionally rotten meat and vegetables were added, a couple of ounces of bread, a tiny amount of margarine, and a bitter drink of tea or coffee.

But after several weeks on starvation rations, the prisoners wasted away to barely-alive skeletons. Weakened by dehydration, hunger, and despair, most inmates quickly fell victim to disease.

I listened to her and was reminded of what Max had told us about outbreaks of lice and contagious diseases in the camps. My back itched. I scratched the side of my neck and moved my hand over my scalp that ached in places where the harsh razor left abrasions.

That night I forced myself to eat the rancid meat and vegetable soup. In survival mode, I willed myself not to dwell on the past. If I opened my heart (even a little) to life before Hitler, I would die of grief or do something to make the Nazis kill me.

The next day, I learned that some of the prisoners worked inside the camp, while others were employed outside: in coal mines, in rock quarries, on construction projects, and, under armed guards, to shovel snow from the roads. A sizeable number were also put to work in munitions and other factories that supported Germany's war effort. Hitler and his inner circle devised a plan for a Thousand-Year Reich or Third Reich. As Max had once explained to me, "Hitler wanted his vision to last a thousand years." And before we Jews were all annihilated, we'd be used as slave labor to help achieve the means to this end.

I was assigned to a women's work detail in the building where we sorted prisoners' clothes, which had been removed upon arrival at the camp. These items would be shipped back to be used in Germany. Still frail, I stood in line folding clothes when, by a stroke of luck, I saw my dress—the one Max had given to me. Quickly, to make it look like an accident, I grabbed it, along with a bundle of other items, and shoved them to the floor. I bunched my dress under the belt of my frock and returned the rest of the garments to the table. For the remainder of the day, I stood hunched over my worktable, trying not to draw attention. I breathed easier once I returned to my bunk where I stashed my dress into a hole in my mattress. I risked my life to get that dress, wanting to reclaim a tiny part of the devastating losses I had endured. That dress also represented the last time I was genuinely happy and felt feminine. There was something mysteriously empowering about the fact that I got away with taking it. No one reported me. If someone did see me, the compassion in her heart outweighed the small reward she might have received.

Touching the dress in my mattress, I felt something stir in me—it was a reminder that, inside the bag of bones I was becoming, a woman still resided.

Chapter Twenty-Five

Days blurred into weeks. Time moved slowly, like a clock with a faulty pendulum. The winter of 1942 edged into spring. I thought about how May used to be my favorite month. Trees grow their leaves. Flowers bloom. It's the time of year when flocks of birds transporting seeds and swarms of bees cross-pollinating were busy creating new life. Yes, May used to be my favorite month; it carried promise and renewal. But after several months in Auschwitz, nothing was fresh. Every morning before dawn we were startled awake by a guard. If we did not make our bed, which consisted of a small threadbare blanket and the mattress, to their satisfaction, we were punished. Punishment usually meant death. The day-in-day-out routine was torture.

Marched out to roll call, we stood in paltry tattered uniforms as the block *kapos* counted the number of captives before reporting to the SS. If the number was incorrect, we stood for hours until it was sorted out.

Anyone not able to stand was carted off to his or her death or killed in front of us. Evening roll calls were the worst. They were usually longer than the morning ones because the SS reviewed each prisoner's performance for the day. We stood, without protection from the weather, as the guards called out our names and either let us step back into line or executed those accused of being lazy, uncooperative, or attempting to escape. Often these charges were false—contrived for the amusement of the sadistic guards.

I remembered a particularly cold evening when an elderly man had fecal incontinence. When he started crying, the officer in charge beat him to death. That roll call lasted all night and included additional beatings. These cruel spectacles became commonplace. There was nothing to do but stand at attention, stare into space, and will my mind to go blank. There were times I pretended it was *just a movie*. Not real. There was no way to take in all the pain and suffering without some mental maneuvering on my part. To emote or allow the reactions in my body—nausea, acid stomach, muscle knotting, aches and pains all over—to be seen would be to raise my hand and say, *kill me*.

Every day, guards in the nine watchtowers pointed rifles as we trudged past the double barbed-wire electric fences. Dogs in the streets had a better life than we did. The end of mealtime was indicated with the sounding of a siren, at which point we'd form into work groups. Marched at gunpoint by SS with automatic weapons and guard dogs, we went to our assigned labor stations.

When I wasn't folding clothes, I cut the linings out of fur coats to look for hidden jewelry or valuables. For twelve hours a day, I handled other's belongings. My heart broke a little more each time I looked at photographs of once happy families, now shattered. I couldn't help but think of my dear family, now lost to me forever and wonder how much more my heart could break.

But there was a balance. Simple things keep me going. The brave, little flower that bloomed in the dry, cracked, unforgiving soil surrounding my barrack was an inspiration to my starving soul. The tiny, yellow petals held their head up high upon the lush, leafy green stem. It was a little miracle that reminded me of how resilient the will to survive in the harshest of conditions can be. There was also the kindness of others. I came to dinner one day, and Ester served me a ladle of soup. She took extra care to dish out a big piece of salami for me. The warmth of the smile on her face softened the cutthroat cruelty of the SS. During that night, she came to my bed and handed me something. Whispering in my ear, she said, "You're around my daughter's age. Today's her birthday. She would have been twenty." She handed me a sizeable piece of bread dipped in margarine. "Don't let anyone see you eating this."

I put the generous gift down for a moment and reached for her. "I love you, Ester. You're my family now." I wept. With every swallow of what she sacrificed to give to me, I cried—not just because of the extra food, but also for the tenderness with which she offered it.

Nothing is ever what you think it's going to be, and that was true with the camp. I imagined that I would spiral into depression, and perhaps death, but I didn't. The atrocities continued, but I created a "survival mentality," allowing me to dull my senses so that I was able to function without collapsing from the mental and emotional burden of living in a death camp. I came to see that Auschwitz exemplified the best and worst of the human condition. The simple, albeit rare, instances of selflessness, and the risky acts of compassion were a healing balm, mending my broken heart. There were those, like my friend Ester, who shared whatever they had—whether it was bread, or a warm blanket, or a shoulder to cry on when they were bone-tired and needed to sleep. They were there for us. I will never forget Clara. She was probably in her forties, about the same age as Ester. Skin-on-bones and hunched over, she gave her blanket to another woman with a cold. "Don't get pneumonia," Clara told the receiver of the gift. Another night, a woman hummed softly to a crying bunkmate until the distraught woman calmed. Those were the angels who lifted us up and inspired me to do what I could even if it was nothing more than offering an understanding smile. Unlike the *kapos*, who sold us down the river for a cup of coffee, they made life a little easier to bear.

* * *

Summer and fall crept into winter. I had been in the camp nearly a year and continued to work sorting clothes. Like the rest of the prisoners, I became emaciated despite Ester's continuing gifts of extra food when possible. I was five feet two inches tall but weighed around ninety pounds. The only part of my body that remained fleshy was my chest. Since puberty, my breasts had been disproportionately large compared to the rest of my body. I tried to hunch over and puff out the top of my dress to hide my bosoms, but the SS knew what I was trying to hide from them. Their stares unnerved me. Although Hitler made it illegal for a German, especially the elite SS, to sleep with a Jew, raping and using women as sex slaves was the rule, not the exception. Rumors circulating the camp warned us which officers to avoid. So far, none of the notorious offenders were on duty where I worked.

Once the last roll call of the day was over, we felt freer to express ourselves in ways that connected us to our humanity—vital after having been treated as subhuman since dawn. Those of us with enough energy danced, sang and told stories. We shared the only thing of value we had left: our memories. I realized that we had created a new family—bonded through devastating loss and grief—to fill the empty spaces inside all of us. We were kin in the most elemental way. For me, our evening gatherings felt like a wake. We honored those who had died with our stories. We prayed. We nodded when someone would whisper, "They wouldn't want us to suffer," or "They would want us to get on with life." Communing with my new family of emaciated prisoners helped me feel human again. I remembered what it felt like to be someone that is seen and heard. A few of my new kin took risks by speaking more loudly than prudent, "To hell with the SS!" Laughter— even if suppressed so we wouldn't attract the guards or *kapos*—helped to release the indescribable stress we endured. Even among our cadre of "trusted ones," we never knew when someone would betray us.

The camaraderie notwithstanding, life in the barrack was difficult. I was always being watched or felt as if I was. Privacy is a luxury of the rich and powerful; I was neither. I expected to be guarded and scrutinized during the day, but having no privacy at night was exasperating. And exhausting. Sleep was imperative to survival, but sleep in a barrack of 300 snoring, weeping, groaning, gassy, incontinent, restless people was a challenge. Lying awake, I also heard noises that surprised me: the sounds of lovemaking and an array of reactions from laughter to disgust from others who, like me, couldn't sleep. The first time I laughed since Ben and I were ripped from Max's farm was a night I heard tiptoe footsteps approaching. "Shush." A man directed his instruction to me and then used my bunk to climb to the one above mine. Before long, I heard suppressed moans and repressed bursts of pleasure from them. Muffling a giggle, I remembered the many nights in the cellar when Ben and I pleasured ourselves. Tears of nostalgia, pleasure, and sadness rolled down my face.

When the man returned several nights later, I wept as my hands found parts of my body yearning to be touched and experience release. My attempt was muted from lack of food, sleep, and most certainly from an unclean body. I was not successful that night. There was no way for me to rid myself of the filth, but that didn't stop me from wanting to feel pleasure from my body—something that is every woman's birthright. That night, determined to maintain my dignity, I decided that I wanted to experience as much normalcy as I could. *The SS will not take my identity as a woman! They will not take my memories, my dreams, or my future!* Huddled next to my dress several nights later, I was able to relieve some of my built-up tension. And it felt good.

Together in the barrack there were those of us who found ways to give purpose to our existence, like the woman who had a few stolen moments of intimacy with the man who snuck in to be with her. How he made it past the guards is something I will never understand. Perhaps they were asleep or otherwise occupied? I like to think their Bible may have played a role, that they turned the other cheek. I wanted to believe that a modicum of goodness prevailed even in the worst of conditions. While some took risks and survived, others with sunken, dark, blank eyes and protruding bones gave up and merely moved on their conveyer-belt life until they succumbed to death.

Something inside of me refused to give up. Was I surviving because I thought I had a future beyond this nightmare? Was I living to keep my family's memory and Max's memory alive? Maybe I was just determined to outlive the demons who put me this hell.

I didn't know why, but, bit by bit, and against all odds an infusion of vitality came back to me.

The Seven Year Dress

Chapter Twenty-Six

A year of my life in the camp vanished. I used to measure the passing of time by holidays and special celebrations with family and friends. Now the changing seasons were measured by the number of clothes I folded, gunshots I heard, corpses I saw, meals I swallowed that weren't fit for a dog, and nightly clandestine gatherings of my new family. One year felt like ten.

Amazingly, I got used to most of the routines in the camp. I could manage trouble sleeping, standing in roll call line for hours, eating slop, and the lascivious looks and comments from the guards that made my skin crawl. I could even deal with having the barrel of a rifle trained on me while standing for hours in the building full of clothes and other's belongings. But what I couldn't handle, what I never adjusted to, was wondering what had happened to the young sons and daughters of families dumped from the trains into the gates of hell. The clothing of the children and babies reminded me of the worst crime against humanity perpetrated by the Nazis. I heard the screams of devastated, sobbing parents. "They carted them off to killing centers and gassed them. Our children!" That was impossible to witness. And I never adapted to the gratuitous killing when an SS officer was in a bad mood and took it out on a poor victim.

My nervous habits continued. While picking at myself was painful, it was familiar, thus comforting. I nibbled my nails down to the quick, and I picked my cuticles raw. It was a miracle my hands never became infected from all the filth in the barrack. No amount of nail-biting or picking at my skin could alleviate the endless distress of trying to survive as a prisoner in Auschwitz. I had constant headaches and a stiff, inflexible tightness around my neck. I also developed a twitch in my left calf that kept me up many nights.

My emotions went up and down like a rollercoaster. Most of the time, I worked mindlessly—like the beat of my heart—when I was dealing with adult clothing articles: the coats, suits, shirts, dresses, shoes, hats, purses, and undergarments. After several months at that workstation, I simply processed the items and wondered if I was becoming callous. I was disabused of that notion when a small dress came to my workstation. Suddenly, all my suppressed feelings—the natural, compassionate, human reactions to this unbelievably heinous situation—flooded to the surface. It was a tiny, wool, plaid baby's dress. Holding the tartan quilled green, orange, and navy blue cloth in my hands, I saw an image of a crying baby. Empathizing with that poor little girl, I felt my shoulders sink into my chest. I remembered how I cried for my Mamma when I was young. She was always there to comfort me, lift me up and rub my back as she whispered, *"There, there, my sweet Helen. You are safe in Mamma's arms."* And I knew, from her touch and gentle words, that it was true. I was safe. Who was there when this plaid dress was ripped from the baby? Who was there to quell her fears when her family was being destroyed? And who was there to offer help to the inconsolable mother and father? Feeling the material of that baby's dress, a lump in my throat threatened to explode. Trying to swallow, I gagged and was hit by panic that I was about to show an emotion that could get me killed. *Breathe. Breathe.* I inhaled the musty odor that came from the stacks of clothing and calmed myself. After that, afraid of being caught daydreaming, I had to curtail my ruminations about the people who once wore the clothes piled in front of me.

This was my life, week after week.

As the year 1943 moved on, I wondered what was happening outside of Auschwitz. Were other countries involved in Hitler's war? How many? Would anyone be coming to free us? Years later I learned that after America had entered the war, carmakers and other manufacturers retooled to produce combat equipment. Even Hollywood was making movies with wartime themes that portrayed Hitler as evil. After I had come to America, I saw a movie with the Three Stooges. The movie was an attempt to alert American audiences to the serious ethical threat of Nazism at a time when many people were still not sure what was going on in Germany.

Despite Hitler's attempts to conceal the atrocities he ordered, the world discovered the truth. Prisoners who had escaped with the help of underground resistance groups spread the word. Brave people risked their lives to smuggle out secret Nazi documents and deliver them to the Allies with pleas for help. But help didn't come fast enough to save the millions of Jews and other victims of torture and annihilation.

With another spring approaching, changes had taken place. Many of the women in my barrack were gone, including the woman who made love in the bed above mine. I missed them. As new arrivals were ushered in and took their places, I saw the looks and demeanor of panic, fear, and shock that mirrored how I felt when I first arrived. I felt strangely satisfied to offer compassion and hugs to those weary from travel and shocked from loss. Easing their pain helped make mine less intense.

The day a young girl, Sarah, came to the camp popped into my mind. She was no more than thirteen, and entered the barrack much like I did: crying and shaking.

I watched her look for an empty bunk. She stopped, put her hands to her shaven head, and turned in circles. Heartache, apprehension, fear, and devastation were written all over her. She didn't know what to do. Neither had I when I first arrived.

I went to her and gently put my hand on her shoulder. "Let me help you."

Her glazed-over, red, swollen eyes focused on me. Unable to utter a sound, she fell in my arms.

"I understand," I whispered in her ear as she clung to me.

When she was able to speak, all she did was moan "Why? Why? Why?"

There was that insufferable word again! My taut neck grew stiffer as the last word Lawrence spoke before he was killed rang in my head. "Breathe," I whispered, trying to calm her. Her delicate upper body rested heavily against my chest, so I knew her breathing had slowed down. She was calmer. So was I as the image of Lawrence eased away. "Good, that's good. A few more deep breaths." I rubbed her back.

Stepping back from my embrace, she was composed.

"My name is Helen. Yours?"

"Sarah."

"Let's find you a place to sleep, Sarah." I glanced away and noticed that Ester had been watching. We shared a knowing look and whisper-soft smile.

My friendship with Ester grew. I gave thanks for her and her companionship every day. Although we were not able to talk much, the affection was ever present in smiles, gentle touches, stolen hugs and a kiss on my forehead in the dark confines of the barrack before we went to sleep, and looks of understanding when tears could not be stopped. I loved my friend, but we had to be careful not to express our mutual fondness overtly. Jealously, greed, and even *schadenfreude* existed among my Jewish barrack-mates.

Our closeness could have prompted someone to try to win favor with the SS by reporting a lie about us. Since informers were rewarded, hunger, weariness, and emotional distress drove a few of the weaker inmates to turn other prisoners in, even if they had to devise false accusations. The Nazis didn't care if the information was fictitious or real. They savored any reason to punish us.

Wanting to help Sarah acclimate, I was distraught when a horrible event occurred in our barracks a few nights after she arrived. After a very long evening roll call, three men slumped to their death, and a fourth man was shot because he attempted to help someone else who was struggling. I stood next to Sarah and, using subtle, stolen glances, tried to keep her focused on her shoes. The SS guards finally released us to our bunks after making us stand still for hours in the bitter cold. I gave Sarah's hand a furtive squeeze—a sign that we were now safe enough. I was wrong.

There was a couple, Samuel and Edith, who favored each other and occasionally risked sleeping together for warmth...and other reasons. On that night, Samuel must have waited until the snores in his barrack grew so loud that he felt it was relatively safe to sneak in and go to

Edith's bed. Shortly after they settled in together, the barrack door flew open. The lights flooded the building, startling everyone awake. Two barbarous, tight-shouldered SS officers entered with their guns drawn. With them was the *kapo*, Saul, from Samuel's barrack.

"Where are they?" the taller Nazi demanded while the shorter one smiled.

Saul pointed to the couple clutching each other.

The short SS officer aimed his gun. *Bang! Bang!* The bullets hit their groin areas. Those heartless Nazi fiends left the two innocent lovers there to bleed to death while we watched in terror. Sarah started to move toward me with a horrified puzzled look in her eyes, the same look she had when she moaned, "why" upon her arrival. I gently shook my head and indicated with my hand for her to stay put. I feared the rampage would continue and we'd all be killed.

When the couple appeared lifeless, the shorter officer motioned to Saul. "Go check their pulse. Make sure the pigs are dead."

A bowing sycophant, Saul said, "Yes, yes," as he lumbered to the motionless bodies. He lowered his shoulders to put his head on Edith's chest, listening for a heartbeat. After doing the same for the Samuel, he shook his head, indicating they were gone.

"Good!" The taller officer smiled and dusted his hands together as if finishing a job. "For your snitching." He threw Saul a piece of stale bread. "Now go back to your barrack."

We all knew that if Saul were harmed, the entire camp would be punished. Samuel and Edith would get no justice. I hated that. I hated explaining that to Sarah even more.

The SS took their time in leaving. I feared that they had changed their minds and would start checking all the beds. When their backs turned, I bit my lip and discreetly made sure my blanket covered the dress Max gave me. After that night, it remained stashed in the mattress.

Before exiting, the tall SS officer ordered us to clean the bloody mess and get rid of the bodies. A few of the stronger women removed the remains of Samuel and Edith to be dumped in one of the mass graves around a kilometer away. Those who carried the couple got no sleep that night. Neither did those of us who cleaned the blood and excrement—all that remained of two human beings.

I spent the rest of the night with Sarah, rubbing her back, letting her cry, and staying by her side when she finally slept. I wanted her to see me when she woke up. She wanted that, too.

Dawn finally broke. Sarah opened her eyes and said, "Bless you, Helen." I knew she'd be okay. For that day she was. I only wished that poor Sarah had been blessed, for several weeks later, unable to contain her emotions in front of an SS officer, she was beaten to death.

Exhausted, the next day—after the execution of Samuel and Edith—I marched to work as usual, but that day would prove to be anything but routine.

Chapter Twenty-Seven

Enervated from lack of sleep, I willed myself not to think about what had happened last night and tried to fold clothes at my normal pace. The SS imposed a daily quota for the volume of garments each prisoner must sort. Falling below the quota was dangerous. As the day moved on, I felt as if I was being watched closer than usual. Glancing at the SS officer who was staring at me, I grew self-conscious and quickly turned my attention back to my work. I struggled to keep focused on my job, but something familiar about him haunted me. Since he had never been in the building before, I tried to figure out where I'd seen him. After a long while, he came closer.

Pretending to be overly involved in the task at hand, I felt his breath on my neck. The fine hairs on my arms stood on end. Something about him and his aggressive proximity made me move my knees together in a protective gesture. I wished that his inspection was only transitory. But when he came even closer, my gut twisted and I could feel my heart

261

pound faster. Harder. Out of the corner of my eye, I caught his eyes scanning my breasts. I blushed. I sorted more quickly. I prayed to God that I could disappear.

"You do a fine job, Fräulein."

When he spoke, I knew where I had seen him. He stood with the SS officer who shot my brother. This scoundrel, this SS monster, did nothing but laugh and joke when my brother was assassinated right before my eyes. And now this! Just as my anxiety level rose to a panic, he put his hand on mine. Nausea clutched my throat, and I took a hard swallow. When he rubbed his hand across my dry, cracked skin in a suggestive manner, I held my breath. I clenched my knees tighter, kept my head lowered, and, fearful of what would happen next, I waited.

"You're the one who sews," he said, removing his hand.

I started breathing again but remained silent and stock-still. *Did he ask me a question or not? Should I answer?* I didn't know what to do and feared that anything I did or didn't do would end badly for me.

When I said nothing, he repeated, "You are the seamstress? Yes?"

Still afraid to speak, I nodded.

He moved his mouth closer to me, his breath now grazing my cheek. "Good." Then, as surprisingly as it all began, he backed off and left.

Looking back on that, I see it was a watershed moment for me at Auschwitz. It was the day when my father's wisdom that "life is precious" and my mother's practicality to "learn a useful trade like sewing" grew from seeds into a tree. And although what was to follow became more of a living hell, I endured and grew stronger. I believed that God was testing my fortitude. Having learned to sew would save my life, but could my heart and soul withstand what my life would become?

That evening, overly exhausted from no sleep the night before and unable to stop the replay from that repugnant encounter with the SS officer, my mind was abuzz. I kept thinking of what Max had told us about liaisons between Germans and Jews being illegal, but I also remembered the rumors that Ester had shared with me. Working in the kitchen, she overheard the slip-of-the-tongue remarks that came from women's hushed-tone venting. In a camp the size of Auschwitz, there were a plethora of men without spouses or girlfriends. Men with carnal urges. I saw that hunger in the eyes of the SS who watched me stripped naked after I arrived. The only women available to satisfy their needs were the prisoners. Sex between Jewish women and the men running the camp—the SS and even the Nazi commanding officers—was illegal but happened all the time. Any doubt I had about the rumors vanished. I knew that officer who visited me had lust on his mind; it was as clear as daylight. But would he act on his impulses, and how would having sex with him impact my life?

Two days later I had my answers when SS officer Claus Schüler returned. He loomed over me, all five feet, ten inches of him. He had a repugnant swine paunch. And he called Jews pigs? Fie! He looked like one himself. He was disgusting to look at with greasy hair and an overly round face that flaunted a tiny mustache, like Hitler's. Just the comparison of the two ogres made my stomach lurch. He found me at my workbench and said he would like to have a word with to me.

A word? What the hell does that mean? I turned to face him, avoiding eye contact and waited for him to speak.

He placed his hand firmly on my back. "Not here," he said as he moved me along the aisle to the exit. I felt sweat forming under the heat of his fat palm as he walked me down a long corridor. We stopped in front of a locked door.

He took out a crowded ring of keys, found the correct one for the small lock and *click!* He pushed the door open. I entered a room approximately ten feet by ten feet. The first thing I noticed was the table with a sewing machine. Nazi uniforms were piled on top of it. A twin-size mattress, a blanket, and a pillow rested on the floor next to the table. He moved to the back of the room and opened another door, revealing a private bathroom. The sink was rusted and filthy, and the toilet looked as if it hadn't been cleaned in months. "How do you like it?" he asked.

Flabbergasted and frightened, I remained silent.

"Sit," he forcefully insisted, pointing to the chair by the sewing machine. He softened his commanding tone and repeated "Come and sit," when I failed to move.

The chair was comfortable and a perfect height for working at the Pfaff sewing machine. I slid my hand over the cold metal of the head and inspected the presser foot, spool pin, pulley, thread needle, and other parts. Closing my eyes, I was momentarily back home in Berlin, mending clothes with Mamma. Schüler made a guttural sound to clear his throat, ending my brief reverie. I looked up and made eye contact with him for the first time. His empty, dark eyes made my blood run cold. "Is this for me to use?" My voice sounded small, child-like.

"Yes. Do you like it?" He licked beaded sweat that had dripped onto his upper lip.

Before the horror of Hitler's regime, I loved to sew; now, I was afraid to enjoy anything that could be taken from me. I didn't want to experience another loss. It was typical of these sadistic Nazis to tempt me with the promise of something pleasant only to rip it away from me and watch me suffer. I had learned never to lose sight of where I was and with whom I was dealing. I politely responded, "It's very nice."

"Good. You now have a new job. You will sew officers' uniforms. And any other items I bring to you. You will work alone here and keep to yourself. No conversations with anyone. You can leave this room for meals and to return to your bunk at night. Your shift time is the same. Do you understand?"

"Yes, sir."

"And," he smirked, "you will do favors for me in return."

My heart sank. There it was, the sexual insinuation. I was trapped. If I refused to work here, he'd kill me; if I agreed, I knew he'd rape me. Either way, my choice was death—literal or figurative. I had always dreamed that my first sexual encounter would be memorable. I imagined tender, loving, warm intimacy with a man I adored—the kind of lovemaking my parents must have enjoyed. I never envisioned rape with someone like him as my first unforgettable sexual experience. I didn't know how or when it would happen. I only knew that my naïve teenager daydreams about romantic love would soon become a nightmare that would scar my soul forever.

The Seven Year Dress

Chapter Twenty-Eight

I knew the gossip would spread quickly when the women I worked with saw Officer Schüler touching me in such a personal way as he escorted me out of the clothing room. When I didn't return to work, the rumors must have been flying. In the barrack that night, I was too scared to talk for fear of being overheard. I didn't want to be seen as someone who was favored by the SS. Hesitant to say anything even to Ester, I avoided her and feigned feeling sleepy. I climbed into my bed, but I couldn't rest. There was no stopping the gibbering going on between my ears. Images of being pinned down by a lecherous monster made my skin crawl. My life had become a Shakespearean tragedy that had taken an ominous turn.

Ester, also unable to sleep, came to my bunk in the middle of the night. "What is it, Helen?" she softly asked.

No longer able to contain the tears I had withheld since the predator first looked at my breasts, I burst out crying. "What gives a man the right to..." I choked out my whispered half-question. With Ester's hand upon mine, my

269

intense, anxious speculations ran rampant. Were Hitler and his band of criminals like Macbeth, who received a prophecy from witches and sank into the realm of arrogance and madness? But where was the guilt and remorse Macbeth felt? I couldn't believe that I was envisioning my life as a Shakespearean play. It felt so unreal. Perhaps it was the only way to help me face what I desperately wanted to avoid. There are people in the world who engage in evil acts without remorse. Indeed, they seem to derive pleasure from making others suffer. And I was under the control of such people. "Ester, I don't want to go to this new job, only to march into the arms of that beast." I covered my face with my hands, ashamed to think about what would surely happen.

"I heard about it," whispered Ester. "Be careful, Helen." She caressed my face and softly kissed my forehead.

Sensing there was more that she wasn't saying, I watched her as she went to her bed. We both knew traitors lived among us, and talking wasn't safe. Although nearly everything that happened in the camp was fodder for reports to the SS in exchange for meager rewards, there was one *verboten* subject the Nazis refused to acknowledge from prisoners: sexual violence. *Rassenschande* laws that prohibited Aryans from having sex with inferior races—especially Jews—didn't stop Nazis from touching and defiling Jewish women. Because such abuses were against the law, they were considered invisible in the camps.

Lying in my bunk, dreading the dawn and my new duties, I remembered Miriam. She was a young, beautiful Jewish girl who was roused from her bunk under some trumped-up reason to do work in the middle of the night. Marched barefoot in freezing weather, her attacker ostensibly told her if she screamed or spoke a word, he would kill her. She was shoved behind a bush and violently raped. The blood from her lost virginity left a stain on her dress, the one she lived and slept in. The next morning, she was visibly subdued and in shock. As we stood in morning roll call, I could see the angry bruises on her body. She couldn't stand up straight. Unable to bear her own weight the three hours in the snow, she succumbed to the pain and fell to the ground. When another woman tried to help her up, they were both shot. Miriam was only fourteen-years-old. Just as I had done with countless other deaths and beatings, I had expunged her trauma from my psyche, until my current threat loomed over me. I could only pray that officer Claus Schüler had an iota of decency in him.

The next day, I took inventory of my new workroom without my captor scrutinizing me. The sewing machine. A pile of uniforms. A basket of thread spools. A fresh, clean towel. A pair of scissors. My first thought was of the blades of the shears buried to the handle in Schüler's back. My shaking hand moved to touch them. I looked around, making sure no saw me eying the scissors. Then I giggled nervously. Even when was alone, I felt as if was being watched! Who had I become? Was this what Papa had in mind when he taught me to stay alive? Attacking an SS officer was insane. I knew if I lifted them in a menacing gesture, it would be the last move I would ever make.

Shaking my head to clear it, I went to check out the washroom. The hot water faucet should have been labeled "cold." I let the wetness run over my hands and arms before picking up a dirty bar of soap to cleanse myself. Deciding I only needed clean hands to avoid soiling the uniforms, I didn't dare to indulge in the luxury of washing my entire body. I noticed the grimy, foul toilet and flushed it. The sludge remained. When a wisp of cool air hit me, I startled. Peering back through the door to the other room, I assured myself that no one had entered. The source of the draft was high above me on the wall; it was a vent. I gently, quietly closed the toilet seat lid with trembling hands and climbed on top for an eye-level view through a louver. My knees knocked together as the jitters spread up and down my body. If Schüler caught me doing this, he'd kill me. What I saw did nothing to calm my fears. Guards were marching prisoners at gunpoint. I quickly got down and went to work. I thought of those prisoners throughout the day, and I wondered if they were in formation, en route to the gas chamber.

Schüler arrived shortly after lunch. With a brusque movement, he opened the door and slammed it shut. He fumbled with the lock until I heard what sounded like metal cracking. He banged a boot loudly on the floor and screamed, *"Scheisse!"*

My heart jumped in my chest.

Pivoting around, he turned toward me. His posture was stiff, and his eyes narrowed. "That will be fixed," he growled at me but pointed a rigid index finger at the door.

Bending my head, I looked down when he approached me sitting at the sewing machine. He lifted my face up with his sweaty hand. "I hope you are making progress with the sewing."

I was sure that the status of the uniform repairs was not foremost on his mind as his wanton fingers moved over my forehead, down a cheek, and onto my neck. Lowering the neckline of my dress, he toyed with my cleavage. I cringed beneath his sticky touch. His drooling mouth moved close to my skin, and I thought I was going to be sick when his saliva dripped onto my chest. Just as liquid rose from my stomach to my throat, he pulled back and barked, "Get up and clean yourself."

While I was in the bathroom, I heard him slide a chair against the door to the outside. Crouching over the sink with my dress still on, I wet the towel and scrubbed my face, neck, and arms. I had begun washing one of my legs when he entered the bathroom, ordering me, "Take off that dirty rag."

Ashamed and embarrassed to do as he commanded, I hesitated. But I knew the consequences of resistance, so I removed my clothing and covered myself with the towel.

Pointing to a hook by the sink, he said, "Put the towel over there." He then stood behind my naked, shivering body and instructed, "Now use that soap."

Trying to calm my hand tremors, I picked up the slimy bar of soap and rubbed it between my hands under the running water. For months, I had dreamed of having a bath—of cleaning myself—but now it was the last thing I wanted to be doing in front of that slovenly beast. The soap burned my cracked, dry skin, but my humility burned hotter than any physical pain. If ever there was a time when I needed to distance myself from reality, this was it.

"Do. Not. Make. Me. Wait."

Each word was a needle in my flesh. I hurried. When I was finished, I wiped myself with the towel.

Sneering, he pointed to my private parts and said, "Decontaminate that rat's nest."

Decontaminate! You horrible, fat, disgusting... *Breathe.* I made myself take a breath and do as I was told. When I'd finally finished, he moved in closer and cupped my breasts with his gummy palms. While still fully clothed, he pumped his groin onto my naked buttocks. I cringed as he freed a hand to undo his pants while his other hand groped up and down my body. Without entering me, he masturbated his male hardness onto my backside. He pounded over and over until I thought my pelvic bone would crack against the sink. Panting, he squeezed my nipples so hard I had to bite my lip to prevent myself from screaming out in pain. Finally, he fell onto me, breathing heavily. After a few seconds, he cleaned himself with a handkerchief and straightened his pants.

"When that damned lock is fixed, I will have you properly."

Have me properly? What the hell did that mean? I spent the rest of that afternoon sewing Nazi uniforms while grieving the loss of my innocence, my captive situation, and the torture I had to endure and would continue to endure until this evil creature was finished using me. I hoped the lock would never be repaired.

It was fixed in three days. I was surprised that the repair wasn't done immediately; my molester was probably busy with other matters. During that limbo, I worked, paced, picked at my cuticles, and tried to remain as calm as possible. I spoke to no one, not even Ester. Although I made an effort, restful sleep eluded me. I decided that the only advantage to being a sex slave was that I was able to wash regularly. And when the oppressive behemoth wasn't violating me, I sewed.

I had no appetite even though I was slowly starving to death. Nervousness had eroded my stomach. Allowing my mind to dwell on what was going to happen once the lock was repaired fueled my anxiety level. I knew my worrying was harming me, but I didn't know how to turn it off. Was there an emotional switch a person could flip on or off, depending on the circumstances? If there was, the Nazis knew where it was, but I didn't. Even if there were such a switch, I wouldn't use it. I would rather endure the suffering than become like them.

The Seven Year Dress

Chapter Twenty-Nine

I lost my virginity to my tormentor on what started out as a frigid day. Working alone in that small, cold room did not allow me the benefit of collective body heat. Goosebumps became a permanent feature of my dry skin as my body tried, but failed, to keep warm. I rubbed my legs together to generate heat, but they refused to stop shivering. I took a risk and put a couple of uniform jackets over my lap to cover my thinly clothed flesh. If I got caught, I would lie. *These are the garments I'm working on, Sir.* I would fib with a clear conscience.

In the middle of sewing damaged lapel folds on an SS officer's uniform, I wondered how both sides came to be ripped. Visions of violence entered my mind: guns exploding into scared victims, dead bodies losing continence, and blood spurting onto those of us forced to watch.

I thought of the recent surge in the number of new prisoners the guards were processing. The gas chambers were working non-stop. Several of the commanding officers were more callous than usual, something I didn't think was possible. Without any semblance of discretion or decency, they took their hostilities out on innocent prisoners. In the past, the SS murdered children en masse in an isolated area, where we were spared from viewing that horror. Mercy was not their objective. The SS did this for their benefit: to avoid panic, which ultimately would have meant more work for them. But now, as Hitler's Final Solution seemed to be escalating, impatient tempers flared from commanders. They ordered their underlings to kill large groups of feeble prisoners in front of freshly dug graves while those spared for labor were forced to watch. We heard of children—screaming and panicked—thrown into those holes. Alive. Guards watched with loaded guns in case any child dared to climb out. They stayed until all the children were dead. If pandemonium broke out among the witnesses, or if able-bodied parents so much as whimpered, they, too, were shot.

Attempting to rid myself of the torment that mere thinking caused me, I shook my head and tried to shift my attention to repairing the torn lapels. When it was no use, I left the sewing machine and climbed atop the toilet seat to look outside. A glimpse of nature—the trees surrounding and hiding the death camp—calmed me. The ache that lived in my heart and the anxiety that filled my belly were ever-present, but pausing to study a tree tended to still the horror film that played in my mind hours after I'd seen or heard about another barbarity. The agricultural land outside the barbed-wire fence had been cleared up to a tree line in the visible distance. I assumed that the farmers who had inhabited the land were evicted to make way for the expansion of the Third Reich. Glancing out to the cleared space up to the area where green leaves sprouted from healthy limbs, I felt my tight muscles loosen. Beyond the barbed-wire fence, beyond the trees, I imagined villages filled with laugher, music, and the aroma of fresh-baked bread coming from kitchens. I glimpsed the dream of my future. As if my brief respite from stress was a warning that I was doing something wrong, I stiffened once again and looked back to the sewing room. It was empty. I scurried back to my work before anyone could discover that I had allowed myself a moment to connect to the outside.

As I was finishing the last few stitches of the jacket I was working on after lunch, Schüler entered and locked the door behind him. His facial expression was pinched as if someone had grabbed him by the hair on the top of his head. His large, bulging, dark eyes fixated on my chest. "Get up, undress, and go wash yourself!" He could have been talking to the wall.

I did as I was told.

He watched. "Go over there." He pointed to the mattress.

Hunched over, naked, humiliated, I followed his orders. Again. *When will it be over? When will he leave me alone to lick my wounds of degradation and cover myself back up?*

He made me stand and watch him strip. His hairy, rotund belly flopped close to his small, hard penis. Lowering my eyes from the revolting sight, a spasm constricted my throat, threatening to shut off my airway. *Breathe,* I willed myself. I waited.

"Lie down on your back." His cold stare seemed odd to me, given the sweat covering his pudgy face. As he watched me get into position, his breathing quickened. "Spread your legs."

I don't know if I was more disturbed by his matter-of-fact tone or the crass command. My eyes widened, and my whole body began to shake uncontrollably.

"Now!"

I jumped. My tremors stopped. I quickly spread my legs. Even though I thought I had complied, he shook his head and said, "Wider. And lift your bottom up."

Again, I did as he instructed. Closing my eyes, I steeled myself, waiting for what was to come.

"Rub your genitals," he panted.

Feeling disgusted while I was moving a hand over my genitals, I peeked one eye open to see what he was doing. He was rubbing his privates while gawking at my privates! He used my extreme vulnerability for his sexual stimulation. I squeezed my eyes shut, attempting to escape into the darkness.

"Open your eyes!"

The disturbing sight of him holding his penis with a loose fist and stroking it, moving his hand up and down the shaft of his swollen member, made me wince. The small lunch of putrid, watery soup rose from my stomach. I swallowed it back down and prayed I wouldn't vomit. I did everything in my power not to cry. Moaning, he quickened his pace and increased the strokes until he closed his eyes and had an orgasm. When he ejaculated onto my body, I wanted to kill the bastard.

Not waiting for further instructions, I closed my legs. Using my arms and hands, I covered as much of my body as I could.

"Not so quick." He was smirking. "That was foreplay." Pointing a finger toward the bathroom, he said, "We're not done." Again, he commanded me to clean myself. This time, it was to rid my body of *his* filth.

Emotionally and spiritually withered, and physically wasted, I returned to the bed of scornful, humiliating dehumanization. He positioned me on my knees, over him, and forced his penis into my mouth. I gagged as he thrust it in and out until he grew hard. Then he grabbed my head, pulling me away from him. He shoved me onto my back, opened my legs, and climbed on top of me. His member was small, but when he inserted himself into me, I felt a ripping pain like nothing I had ever experienced. I wanted to yell for him to stop hurting me. To stop using me. I wanted to bite and kick him off of me; instead, I remained submissive, letting him have his way with me. The flesh-tearing, searing-hot pain continued for what felt like an hour. Close to unconscious when he got off, I didn't move until he left the room without saying a word. Blood oozed down my legs as I struggled to the bathroom, where I proceeded to vomit the scant liquid in my stomach. When nothing was left, I dry-heaved till my ribs hurt. I felt like I had been pushed off a ten-foot building and landed on concrete. *I wish you were dead! You cold-hearted bastard! You disgusting criminal!*

Traumatized and battered, I scrubbed the insides of my thighs to get whatever was left of him off of me. I rubbed myself raw until every last trace of my stolen innocence was gone. At least I didn't need to worry about getting pregnant. I had malnourishment to thank for not having a menstrual cycle in ten months.

I spent the rest of that day in a fog, going through the motions until I could get in my bunk that night. I curled into a tight ball in a futile attempt to protect myself from the living incubus that had entered my life. I woke up the next day. I stood at attention during roll call. I ate the swill they served. I sewed. I persevered, waiting in a state of eternal dread for the next time he would barge through the sewing room door.

Several days passed until he returned again, but this time, he didn't come for sex. He beat me for not sewing a button on tightly enough.

My relationship with Schüler had evolved. I was the person on whom he took out all of his aggressions, sexual and otherwise. If I sewed one stitch out of line, I was beaten ruthlessly. When he came early and had to wait for me to finish a sewing job, he berated me. "You're a lazy whore." Standing over me, he looked down with a scornful contempt on his tight mouth. "Can't you do your work on time?" He grabbed hold of the back of my neck and pulled me close to his waistline. "No lunch for you today." He smashed the back of his right hand across my left cheek with such force I nearly fell off the chair. "And the next time I come for the sewing have it ready on time, or you'll not eat for a day!" The whiplash effect of that beating left me with a stiff neck for days.

The monster enjoyed torturing me—dismantling my personhood, my womanhood. On some days, when he was in a "good mood," he entered the sewing room and threw a piece of stale, moldy bread at me. I thought he was revealing some glimmer of humanity. I knew I was wrong when he said, "You're lucky to have this arrangement with me." Laughing, he continued, "You get extra food, and you are allowed to stay alive. A stroke of good luck for you."

I didn't know I could hate a person so much.

Although I wanted to vomit everything he offered, I forced myself to eat and stay as robust as possible. I clung to the hope that, one day, I would be free. One day, with this horrendous chapter of my life behind me, I prayed that more than my body would be free—I prayed for the fortitude to embrace life again. I thanked God for Ester, who continued to keep me sane. Her selfless acts of compassion and kindness saved my life. I often called her *mein engel*. Aside from my family and Max, she was the best friend I ever had.

That year was the worst one in the camp for me. I silently begged God to protect me from Schüler's brutal rapes that left painful sores on my vagina and rectum. I never knew what pain was until he roughly entered me and then continued to find new ways to satisfy himself using my body. I couldn't stand the thought of him.

My spirit, bruised and scarred as much as my body, withstood his abuse, never knowing when the day would bring sexual abuse, physical abuse, emotional infliction of pain, or some combination of degradations. I relished the days when he chose to leave me to my sewing, but I never knew when those days might come. So every day I suffered the crippling anxiety of uncertainty; in that way, he was with me even when he was away.

Days, weeks, months passed. Just when my resolve to continue living that way was nearly depleted, fortune shined upon me. The day of reckoning happened in early 1944. Schüler was on evening roll call duty when an elderly man standing near me collapsed. Schüler's eyes narrowed as he pointed his Gewehr at the man and shouted at him to get up. Schüler's neck muscles bulged, and his sweaty face turned red before it became pasty. Dropping the rifle, he grabbed his left arm and stumbled backward. The other guards were too far from him to take notice. Along with other prisoners, I watched his breathing become erratic as he lumbered off, calling for a physician. Medical help arrived too late. Claus Schüler, notorious sexual miscreant and violent abuser of human rights, died face down in the dirt in Auschwitz in February 1944.

At last, one of my wishes had come true.

Chapter Thirty

Although I felt relief at Schüler's death, I was exhausted from months of abuse from that morally bankrupt bastard. I had existed like the ghost of a dead person when around him, suffering what he dealt me as if I wasn't really there. I was determined not to give up; to do that would have let him win. I became mechanical in doing what he asked of me and endured without showing thought or spontaneity. That painful conditioning stayed with me in the camp and for years after. Although he never conquered my soul, he tortured my body and wore me down. After what I had gone through with him, I didn't know how long I could survive Auschwitz. I didn't know a lot of things: would someone worse replace him, and, if so, what would happen to me? On top of everything that had happened, the ambiguity was grueling.

Ester did what she could to lift my spirits, and I had to wonder if she forfeited some of her meals to keep me alive. My sewing job, which I was allowed to continue, was also a lifesaver. I had no energy left in me to stand for twelve hours a day sorting clothing, so sitting at the sewing machine helped me conserve what little energy I had.

As time passed, my body healed in small, but noticeable ways. More apparent, however, was my renewed optimism for life. Day by day, as Ester smiled and kissed my forehead goodnight, my resolve to survive this horror returned. My conviction that a good life was possible—that I might someday be free and happy—evolved slowly, like ocean waves edging over the sand. Without the pervert's daily threat weighing down my spirit, the seeds of resilience living in my soul sprouted once again.

In the middle of 1944, something happened that strengthened my determination to outlive Auschwitz. A light drizzle fell in the night air as two prisoners walked to roll call formation. The one without shoes limped while the other, unfaltering, walked beside him, wearing the wooden clogs handed out to prisoners. The unsteady prisoner cried out in pain and stopped to take a rock out of his bleeding left foot. His companion in clogs also halted. Just as the man with the shoes took them off to give to the other man, an SS guard swooped down on them. Both prisoners were beaten so badly that they were unrecognizable. The guard laughed at his handiwork. My gripped fists turned white as

I watched that crazed beast cackle with sick amusement. They were pummeled to near death because of benevolence.

I wanted to scream, "Stop this madness!" Instead, I held my breath and stood still. I might have looked passive, but inside, I was defiant. I swore I would not succumb to their heinous corruption of all that is sacred and humane. They would not have the pleasure of laughing over my dead body.

As my hatred of Nazis intensified, my compassion for the prisoners blossomed. Virtuous deeds abounded, and I took notice: the man willing to give up his shoes, Ester's sharing her food at great risk to her well-being, others assisting the fallen despite a risk of being shot, and those offering solace to others in emotional turmoil while sacrificing much-needed sleep. These kind, selfless men and women captured my heart and infused my soul with hope that goodness would prevail. Perhaps it was the trauma of being abused in every way possible and surviving it that had changed me. I was no longer the innocent Helen, fantasizing about a joyful marriage with children and a dog. That child, that young woman, was gone, and a new gentle woman was resurrected in her place. I loved the new Helen.

Still, my life was in constant danger, and I remained vigilant. For the past two years in Auschwitz, I stayed alert to strange noises, slept uneasily, and constantly tried to suppress disparaging images and emotions. When I look back on what had happened, I can't explain how I stayed alive. I like to believe that my fortitude came from my parents. That the best of them lived on in me. I saw their altruism shine through me when, like Ester, I shared my food with someone near death from malnourishment. I gave up my blanket to a woman who had a nasty cough so she wouldn't get pneumonia. By helping others when it was safe to do so, I found serenity in the midst of the madness.

Surprised and grateful, I remained in the sewing room, repairing uniforms and articles of clothing that a new guard brought to me. I didn't expect that I would stay on there after Schüler died since the room was a private facade for his sexual exploits. Oddly, and in death, the irony turned on him. Schüler selected me to do the sewing so he could have a sex slave. While he was alive, I wasn't considered a very productive seamstress. Now that he was dead, I was a valued worker, and the quality of my sewing kept the SS from harassing me.

My new guard, Karl Schmidt, was younger than Schüler by probably fifteen years. Perhaps in his late twenties, he reminded me of Max with his strikingly handsome face, straight blond hair, and tall, thin stature. His blue eyes were soft when he spoke to me, and, although he tried to hide his gentle disposition, my heart felt his innate kindness. He was a good person in a bad circumstance. Although he appeared randomly with more uniforms for me to mend, he left me alone for most of the day.

Schüler's death, the welcomed change in Schmidt's disposition, and the innumerable transformations that my life had made in the past three years reinforced something Ester had cryptically said to me the first year I arrived, "Nothing lasts." When I asked her to explain, she only nodded her head. Now I understood.

Despite the difference in the personalities of my former and current guards, when Schmidt entered the room I still flinched into a bundle of twisted muscles. For all of the prisoners, existing in the concentration camp meant the possibility imminent death. I never knew what or who would come through that door. I had been conditioned like one of Pavlov's dogs. I had learned about Pavlov and his Nobel Prize in Physiology before I was banned from school. His work was never clearer to me than when I encountered the bad fortune of negative conditioning at Auschwitz. My new hair-trigger reflexes, my body's involuntary reactions to stress and pain, were etched into my core. An opening door, a loud footstep, a strange noise in the night, a tap on my back, and even laughter like the kind I heard when my brother Ben was executed sent me into a panic. Operating on an abnormal anxiety level day in and day out, I was never far from losing my mind. Perhaps understanding some of the suppressed and subconscious mechanisms at play helped me cope. My responses were normal given the conditions. This knowledge was such a relief.

"I brought you these." Schmidt handed me three uniforms and a dress.

Feeling slightly safer with him, I spoke. "A dress?"

"It seems you have made an impression on the Commandant's wife." Stories had gotten around that I was a gifted seamstress.

"But it's a child's dress," I queried as I held the beautiful beige satin and lace material in my hands.

"It's Brigitte Höss' birthday dress. It was ripped playing with her brother. I'll wait while you repair it. One mistake could be very bad for you."

"Very bad" was an understatement. Commandant Rudolf Höss made an art of treachery. He blithely ordered the torture and deaths of thousands of prisoners—including children—while doting on his own children in his off-camp mansion. Prisoners overheard stories that the SS told about the Commandant as a loving father and husband. I knew about him from Ester. While Höss lived in luxury, we lived in squalor and rodent-infested dwellings. While he ate the best food available, prisoners ate Salmonella-contaminated meat. Höss resided in a villa with his wife and five children while our families were slaughtered at his command. For a brief time, Commandant Arthur Leibehenschel replaced him, but in May 1944, Höss returned to Auschwitz. His return brought the darkest time to the camp when over 400,000 Hungarian Jews were killed in 56 days. Unable to handle the plethora of corpses, Höss ordered his officers to burn the bodies in open pits within eyesight of horrified prisoners.

My stomach knotted into a painful mass at the mention of the Höss name; I felt as if I had just listened to my death sentence. "Yes, sir," I replied as I looked at the damage. On the back of the dress, above the hem, I examined a rip about six inches long. Her brother must have grabbed it from behind while the girl tried to get away. *Yes, I know the feeling of wanting to flee.* I had thread that matched and felt the best solution was to raise the bottom. I prayed I'd do a good job, and that my hands wouldn't sweat and damage the material. *Didn't these rich Nazis have a personal seamstress? Why trust such an important job to a prisoner? I can't have survived all this time only to be killed for a botched sewing job!* With these thoughts racing through my head, I worked as quickly as I dared while being as precise and careful with the delicate material as possible. When finished, I gently folded the dress to avoid creases and handed it back to my guard.

Alone again, my nervous gut didn't calm until I saw Schmidt hours later when he marched me to roll call formation. He made no mention of the dress. Since I continued to be used for sewing, the repair must have met with the Commandant's wife's approval. To my relief, I never received another garment from the Höss family.

Chapter Thirty-One

As the weeks in 1944 advanced, rumors ran rampant among the prisoners that Germany was losing the war. Ester told me about three of the prisoners who worked in a munitions factory who had overheard a radio listened to by an SS guard. A British station! In hindsight, I wondered if that guard was not a true believer of Hitler's propaganda. Or perhaps he was like my Max—a decent man with his own secrets. Ester also listened as guards, drunk with schnapps, boasted about forty-six people at the camp who had been sentenced to death for listening to foreign radio against Hitler. It was a crime for anyone to listen to a foreign radio station that condemned Hitler's government; their murders for simply listening to the radio, however, were not criminal. Everything about the camp life seemed upside down.

"Could it be true? About Germany losing the war?" I whispered to Ester, trying to tamp down the spark of hope igniting in me.

She shrugged. "The guards said the radio reports were all lies. But the way they said it...I don't know. With the guards, you never know." Ester's words were buoyed up with optimism when she whispered in my ear, "It was as if that guard in the munitions factory wanted the prisoners to overhear...Why? I don't know. If word got out, he would have been killed for it. Perhaps it's the nature of the news and just an attempt for the guard to appear neutral? Who can know another's motives? But," she patted my back and moved her mouth closer to my ear, "I have a good feeling about it."

In a low, hushed tone, I asked, "Do you know what they overhead?"

"Something about an earlier Casablanca Conference that was attended by the United States, the British, and someone from France..."

Years later, when I was reading about the events surrounding World War II, I learned more about the conference that had taken place in January 1943. Attended by United States President Franklin D. Roosevelt, British Prime Minister Winston Churchill, and, representing the Free France Force Generals, Charles de Gaulle and Henri Giraud, it produced a statement of the Allied tactical will:

unconditional surrender of the Axis Powers, which included Germany.

But there, in my bunk, I heard Ester tell me, "I think the Allies are advancing. We are going to be freed, Helen!"

Fearful someone would overhear us, I gritted my teeth and squeezed her hand. In the softest tone I could muster, I breathed, "I pray to God you're right."

"Yes." Ester kissed my forehead and went to her bunk.

I went about my work in Auschwitz with that conversation repeating in my head like a Mozart symphony.

As the hearsay about our liberation lingered, the atrocities continued. Each day was a pins-and-needles paradox: more rumors of Germany's defeat combined with an unmistakable escalation of brutality and murder. At a meal, I overheard whispering men huddled together out of earshot of the guards. They mentioned the Warsaw Ghetto Uprising that had happened last year. Ester had heard more than I was able to comprehend fully. That night, once again, I entreated her to tell me what she knew. She whispered to me, "A man named Jacob Gottlieb arrived yesterday. He escaped the uprising and had been in hiding…"

A cough a few beds over startled me. I put my hand over Ester's mouth and waited. The cough continued a few more times and then quieted down into deep-sleep breathing. "Come closer," I told Ester.

"Apparently the Nazis made the poor Jews living in that ghetto an example of what they do to resisters. That's all you need to hear." She motioned to give me a good night hug and kiss.

"Ester, please, tell me." I held my breath.

Ester sorrowfully shook her head.

"Please." I squeezed hold of her hand.

She let out a deep sigh and put her lips back to my ear. "Jacob and a few others somehow managed to escape, go into hiding, and join up with the another resistance movement. But, by then, it was too late. Many died. Too many perished," she sniffed.

Much later, I learned that the Warsaw uprising was the final effort of an organized Jewish resistance taking place. The single largest revolt by Jews during World War II resulted in 13,000 Jewish deaths—many burnt alive or suffocated.

People in my life had always wanted to protect me from ugly truths: Papa, Max, and now Ester. For me, not knowing was worse than knowing. I didn't need to be protected as much as I needed to be informed. I wanted to know what was happening in *and* out of the camp. In some small way, knowing made me feel as if I still belonged to the world that existed outside of Auschwitz.

The rumor mills were buzzing with contradictory stories. "Germany is stronger than ever!" "Germany is about to be crushed!" Without seeing any variation in my daily life, I began to doubt the news of our imminent freedom. Hope is a dangerous emotion when life is nothing but ambiguity. To avoid becoming depressed, I focused on my sewing.

As new families arrived, I continued to witness the deception. From the sign on the gate promising salvation to those who worked hard, to the enticement of a "shower" for hygiene, on went the lethal lies. As the year progressed, the gas "shower" chambers were operating day and night. The relentless smoke spewing sacred ashes of the dead descending on the camp like a fog that never lifted. It sickened me to feel like I was breathing in dead people. And with every breath I prayed for their souls. I prayed for mine. For Ester's. For Shana's. And I prayed that the cruelty would end.

But the cruelty didn't end. New arrivals, exhausted from days of travel, quickly learned that to sit down meant to be shot. To not obey an order was a death sentence. And so they arrived at the barracks shaken and shocked. I, along with Ester and the other kindhearted prisoners, tried to offer whatever support we could: a listening ear, a warm hand, a gentle hug, or perhaps encouragement like, "You may find your family and be reunited. Don't give up hope."

In that cataclysmic camp of doom, surrounded by many layers of barbed-wire fence, we continued to march to morning roll call, to march to eat, to march to work, to march to evening roll call. We marched by the fallen and dead, and we marched back to the barracks. The nighttime continued to bring respite and signs of life: the gentle comforts of lullabies and old folk songs, the light tiptoe dancing, whispered jokes and storytelling, sweet conversations, and risky lovemaking. Each night before I went to sleep, Ester hugged me and kissed me on the forehead, and then I prayed I'd live to find my sister. The benediction of those moments kept me going another day. And the determination to survive that I saw in the eyes of other prisoners inspired me. I resolved not to give up hope, no matter what.

It was that resolve that had helped me when the vilest of men arrived at the camp, Dr. Joseph Mengele. The minute I saw that cold, calculating, evil face, my heart constricted. When he smiled, no, sneered, a gap between his two front teeth made him look simultaneously diabolical and idiotic. And he constantly smiled when working with his favorite test subjects: children. *How could a human being who conducted agonizing clinical experiments on live children smile all the time?* To this day, I have nightmares about the research he did on infants and children. I had seen children playing in the "nice play-yard" Mengele constructed for them. Ester told me that these children were his experimental subjects. "Out he'd come with sweets for them. They would be so happy! The next minute, a lethal injection, beating, shooting, or selection for deadly research." Ester didn't cry often, but she sobbed when she said, "What he did to those poor youngsters…His evil, uncaring eyes made me shiver." That was the only night that our conversation ended with my dry heaving. I moved even that conversation into the archives of my mind, where I locked up all of my painful memories—neither gone or forgotten, just apparitions that haunt me still when I allow myself to be vulnerable to them.

So life continued as 1944 moved into autumn. I sewed and worked hard at remaining alive and sane. I was lucky that I hadn't made any mistakes to compromise my life. As the rumors intensified that the Allies' breath moved closer and closer to Auschwitz's gate, the prisoners' routines continued. In hopeful moments, I envisioned the victors at our door. What would they think when they came upon living skeletons, some who were despondent and some who were unhinged? Would they understand that the Nazis treated us like animals, not humans? Would they comprehend the atrocities that occurred at Auschwitz, that the entire purpose of the camp was for extermination?

Would the world find out that we labored twelve hours a day, took brief periods for small meals of rotten food, and spent the rest of the time in roll call lines and in our barracks surrounded by filth, vermin, insects, and lice? We bore the scars of their unthinkable acts of indecency and immorality on human rights. We were brought to our knees as they humiliated us for their entertainment. Would the world learn of the Nazi machine's barbarity?

Some like to believe there were lessons to be learned from this moment in history; I disagree. I came to realize that life is a game of chance that you enter. It is up to you to determine how you react to the events that chance presents to you. It is up to you to proceed at your own risk. Is there a God guiding any part of the journey? I don't know. I made it out alive, but what of the millions of innocent souls who didn't? Where was God for those unfortunate victims?

Soon, I wouldn't have to wonder about what the world would think of Auschwitz and the people—dead, alive, and in between—that they found there.

The Seven Year Dress

Chapter Thirty-Two

In mid-January 1945, a huge commotion broke out in the camp. Thousands of detainees were rounded up by the SS and forced to proceed west from Auschwitz on foot. Before the marches, thousands of others were liquidated. Countless rows of prisoners were lined up, shot, and left in open graves. A few, pretending to be dead, hid among the fallen bodies. The sickening bang of each bullet riveted my body. I stood beside Ester in abject terror, biting my lower lip and barely breathing until the SS passed us by. I had no idea why we had been spared. Letting out a breath and still scared to death, I mumbled to Ester, "Do you know what's happening?"

With a trembling hand, she wiped the sweat beading on her forehead. "I think it may have something to do with the gas chambers not working. But I'm not sure."

"The gas chambers aren't working? Why not?" I couldn't believe I was asking that question.

Ester ran her hand over her head. "Last year. Remember? The crematoriums were dismantled. Don't bother asking why. I don't know." She took my hand and squeezed it.

Remembering when they demolished the buildings where they incinerated bodies, a chill ran down my spine. Instead of gassing and burning the poor victims, the SS was now shooting them by graves. *What's going on?* I wondered about the reason for the extensive exodus and why so many able-bodied workers were being killed. But all I could do was watch and wait because Ester's information only went so far.

That Ester and I were not among those to be escorted out the gate of hell proved to be fortuitous. I later heard about those who were decamped. If anyone lagged behind in the line or could not continue, they were shot. Prisoners suffered in the cold winter weather without any protection from the elements, many dying from exposure and starvation. It's estimated that more than 15,000 perished on those marches.

When the last of the groups marching out were gone, the camp quieted. There were still several thousand prisoners and some guards left behind, but thousands upon thousands had exited. Just when we thought the chaos was ebbing, complete disorder and confusion erupted. Flammable liquid was poured over the bodies in the graves and over buildings: the gas chambers, officer quarters, medical buildings, and the research buildings. Lit torches set the bodies and buildings on fire. I heard a loud explosion. I assumed that a gas leak caused the explosion. The SS scampered around frantically, either shooting anyone in sight or throwing papers onto the burning pyres in the death pits.

Ester grabbed my hand. "Run!"

We made it to a relatively safe hiding place under a coal bunker where I overheard an SS officer shout, "The Commandant wants all evidence destroyed!" I deduced from all the panicked yelling that Rudolf Höss and his men were attempting to conceal the mass murders and other evils that had taken place at Auschwitz. "Everyone is to be shot and burned! Leave no one alive." A senior SS officer ordered several younger ones. He appeared to be the one in charge, but he was instantly distracted by other commands flying at him. In the pandemonium to hastily destroy evidence and abandon camp, the remaining prisoners, including Ester and me, were overlooked. Perhaps a junior

SS guard noticed Ester and me hiding but decided to let us live. I'd like to believe that not all Nazis were evil. Maybe we were just lucky.

Huddled together in the cold, Ester and I didn't dare move. For hours, we listened to continued screaming, boots pounding the ground, and trucks being loaded with the files that hadn't been burned. As the smell of burning flesh and paper permeated the air, I heard car doors slamming and engines revving. Ester and I looked at each other with, I think, the same question in our wide eyes: "Are the Nazi monsters escaping from their own death camp?" We remained there, hugging each other until nightfall came and brought with it an eerie quiet. As the moon glistened in the sky, we saw others who had been in hiding get up and walk about in a bewildered state.

Ester tightened her grip on my arm. "Are you ready?"

"To go over there?" I nodded toward a few men standing nearby. Still skittish, I didn't want to move. I feared that this entire episode was just another elaborate, vicious ploy to torture us.

"Yes," she whispered.

"I want to wait. I don't trust…"

"I understand. Then we'll wait," she said.

And we did.

Over the next few hours, more prisoners came out of hiding. I heard some talk of going to their beds to rest. Others came into view with bits of food. When I saw these prisoners moving about freely, talking above furtive whispers, and with food, I was stunned. No one looked over their shoulders; there wasn't a hint of retribution.

"I'm ready," I told Ester. As I listened to the sound of my full voice for the first time in three years, I smiled. I breathed deeply. As the crisp, fresh air filled my lungs, I stood beside Ester and looked around at the remains. Approximately 7,000 Auschwitz prisoners were abandoned by the Nazis, most of us too weak and ill to move. With the unknown looming like a guillotine blade ready to drop, I remained on edge as I did what the others did: slept, foraged for food and blankets, and stared at the sky, wondering what would happen next. Our conversations centered on questions without answers.

On January 27, 1945, our answers came. I heard a man bellow in broken German, "You are free! Come out!" The Russian allies, our liberators, had arrived. The ill, skeletal, wailing prisoners surrendered to men in uniforms who witnessed the sight of the walking dead with their mouths agape and looks of utter shock. I noticed several of the soldiers shaking their heads and wiping tears from their cheeks. Hugs, cheers, kisses, embraces, and "Thank God," sang from the men wearing tattered stripes and women in rag dresses. The Russian soldiers must have wondered how any of us had the energy to move, let alone celebrate our liberation. I often wonder the same thing.

One tall soldier, his eyes moist and his chin trembling, came to me with his hand extended. I looked into his kind eyes and then down to his opened palm. A bar of chocolate. He waited with his outstretched arm as I hesitantly walked toward him. I must have looked like a stray dog. He was using a lure to help me feel safe as he approached me. Glancing up again to meet his benevolent eyes, I fell to the ground and cried. He knelt beside me, opened my palm, and placed the candy in it. Although I couldn't understand the Russian words he spoke, the compassion in his voice told me what I needed to hear.

We were free.

I was free.

The first thing I did with that freedom was to let out seven years of grief that I had swallowed. Before leaving

Auschwitz, I retrieved the dress Max had given me and clutched it to my heart.

Although Höss and his men tried to hide their crimes, nothing could conceal the truth of their torture and mass murder. To the Russians and the rest of the world, evidence of the atrocities, corruption, and the felonious nature of their violations of human rights were evident and inexcusable. I later learned that, while the Russians were at our gate, the British, Canadians, Americans and French troops freed prisoners in other camps. The Germans also failed to hide their crimes in those camps, and the evidence confirmed the enormity of their heinous acts. The legacy of Hitler's grand plan? Millions of dead bodies stacked up like firewood and tens of thousands of prisoners who were walking skeletons.

Allied troops, aid workers, and physicians tried to tend to those left alive. Many were too weak to digest food and died after they were liberated. Nearly half of the prisoners freed at Auschwitz and other camps died despite valiant attempts to save them. Although it was quite some time later, I learned that my sister, Shana, was among those unfortunates who died at Dachau.

Still in a state of shock and programmed to wait for orders or be punished, I remained by Ester's side like an abused animal clinging to the one safe thing I knew. Constantly being hyper-alert and overly suspicious began to hinder the care I was getting to stabilize me for travel to a more secure place. My stomach was constantly upset, I had pounding headaches, and my habit of picking at my skin escalated. Finally, after a couple of weeks of eating healthy food, sleeping on a real mattress, being out in the fresh air, and free to take walks, Ester and I made it out of Poland to an American-run Displaced Persons Camp in Germany.

Ester found a cousin who she went to live with. On our last day together, I had a lump in my throat and a heavy, sorrowful pain in my heart. There was no easy way to say goodbye to my beloved friend. We tried to find words to let each other go, but every attempt at a final adieu failed. So like the many nights we shared in the barrack, Ester silently hugged me and kissed my forehead. For the last time, she wiped the tears from my eyes as rivers streamed from hers. The wisdom and love that united us remained unspoken and unbroken.

With the help of the Red Cross, I went into a relocation program in the United States where I found work as a seamstress.

Before leaving Germany, I managed to visit the bombed-out buildings and rubble that Berlin had become. A few homes on the street where I lived, including my home, were still standing. I stopped by and found a German family living there. They let me in to look around. The house was empty when the new family moved in, and they had no idea what had happened to our belongings. I was the only remaining proof that my family ever existed. If they were to live on, it would be through me—in my thoughts and in my heart.

Max's old home was also intact, a new family living there. His parents had been killed after their son was branded a traitor for assisting a Jew. Devastation and grief rippled through innumerable lives during the debacle of Hitler's regime, and for decades following the liberation.

Throughout 1945, the Allies freed the Jews, and the SS fled. Wanting to avoid the comeuppance they deserved, they disguised themselves; they left the country, and they went underground and crawled away like a pack of fleas on a mangy dog. The deplorable cowards knew their fate should they be caught. The biggest coward—the evilest man of them all, Hitler—took the easy way out. On April 30, 1945, he committed suicide. It was the day after Germany surrendered.

To this day, a part of me is still a prisoner. I remain a victim of the memory and images created by the heartless monsters that wanted to rid the world of the Jewish race. But that is just a small part of me, for my heart has learned to, once again, soften. To trust. Thanks to Ester, the selfless people I met along the way, and the kindness of our decent liberators—those who risked their lives to save mine—I have been able to construct a meaningful life after seven years of torment.

My father was right when he said, *"Life is what's important."*

Epilogue

Present Day

Helen's eyes glistened with overflowing tears as she told me that, after coming to America, she corresponded with Ester. Ester found peace and lived a simple life with her relatives, helping with meal preparation, gardening, and babysitting the young ones as they came into the world. "For a long time, Myra, it was those letters that kept me going. And then my work here. The sewing and kind people I did jobs for helped me grow new roots. I made a couple of friends with whom I'd share meals. They were lifesavers for me when Ester's letters…stopped…, and I knew she had died. She lived well into her sixties. I never made contact with her family after that."

Not knowing what to say, I said nothing. My thoughts drifted from what Helen had told me to her life before

Hitler and the insanity began. There was one person she hadn't mentioned. If by divine intervention, Helen wiped her face, blew her nose, and told me that, after settling in California, she tried to locate Isaac. He was her last connection to Berlin. To her past.

"Did you ever find him?" Waiting for her answer, I glanced around her apartment—at everything in its proper place and aligned just so. Instantly, I understood why nothing was messy or disorderly. She was beaten within an inch of her life if she didn't sew buttons on neatly or keep hems straight. She had to abide by the anal-retentive directives of her criminal captor, the one who raped and abused her week after week, for months on end. I no longer saw my friend, Helen, as a neat freak or some kook bordering on being obsessive-compulsive. This extraordinary woman had been tortuously programmed to act as she did. In relaying her story, she reminded me about Pavlov's experiments about conditioning on canines. Just like a dog does, she learned the behavior that avoided punishment. Although the physical cruelty ended long ago, the mental scars from the kind of trauma she withstood probably never went away. At least now she seemed free to process the ordeal, and maybe some of the pain. All labels I

318

erroneously constructed about her dissolved as she shared her personal history with me. She told me a horror story that opened my heart. I was finally able to appreciate this incredible woman sitting before me.

"Isaac? Yes, we spoke by telephone. He told me that, after we lost touch, he continued with school and became a World History teacher in New Jersey. He met a girl. They married and had two children." She continued to tell me that she withheld the terrible events of her life from Isaac. "I wanted to spare him. It's best to have happy memories. The truth isn't always good to know." She gave me a warm smile. "I suppose Papa, Max, and Ester were right all along."

I took in a deep breath to try to release the tension pressing in on my belly. I wanted to think of something to say, something appropriate, but at a loss for words, I continued to sit quietly with my watery eyes upon hers.

Rubbing her wrinkled hands together, she looked at me and shrugged her shoulders. "I've never spoken the whole story to anyone. And now...all of this to you, Myra." She nodded. "It's good. For some reason, I'm not surprised. Perhaps because you are going to be a nurse?"

A warm flush permeated my body as the generosity of her words flowed through me. For several minutes we sat together silently, looking at each other, and then I opened. "I'm so honored to know you. And I can't thank you enough for trusting me with what happened." I looked around her apartment, again, thinking about what Schüler did to her. Melancholy overwhelmed me. My heart physically ached.

"No, my dear, thank *you*." Her soulful eyes locked with my tearful eyes. Then, smiling a more serene smile than I had ever seen her give, she tilted her head from one side to the other, as if recognizing someone familiar from a long time ago.

Overcome with a compelling urge to hug her, I asked. "Anything else you wanted to say?"

"I remembered something Ester told me on her daughter's birthday. She had said that I was around her daughter's age. I just looked at you and felt what Ester might have felt. If my life were different and I had married, I might have a daughter your age right now." Helen looked past me, wistfully, a little sad. And with a deep sigh returned her gaze to mine, she gently smiled.

A lamp in the room flickered. Both Helen and I looked toward the lamp and to what was sitting next to it: the framed piece of cloth, which was all that remained of the dress Max had given her. That tiny relic was Helen's only tangible link to her origins and the people who she once loved. In that small apartment that day, she glowed when she said, "For many years, I felt that that piece of material, with the blood of my brother splattered on it, was all that was left. For seven years of captivity, from when I went to Max's farm in 1938 until I was liberated from Auschwitz in 1945, that was all that survived of my personal belongings. It was a symbol of everything that had been taken from me. For many years, I believed that." She pointed to the words on the plaque, *Nothing Lasts*. "I was wrong to think that was all that was left." She reached her hand across to mine and gave it a gentle pat. "There's so much more," she smiled. "There's love."

You never know a person until you hear his or her story. Stories change how you feel about someone. When I saw Helen's arm branded with a concentration camp number, I assumed her story wouldn't be a good one with a happy ending. But as I looked into her beautiful, shining eyes, I knew I was wrong. Her spirit lives strong. She is content, grateful to have survived.

I glanced back at what Helen called the *seven year dress*, the gift from Max. I had been curious about those soiled marks. Now, I had my answer.

Perhaps they began as Ben's blood, but they came to be her lifeblood.

Post Note

On 24 October 1945, the United Nations (UN) was established. Replacing the ineffective League of Nations, the UN is an intergovernmental organization to promote international co-operation.

On 10 December 1948, the UN General Assembly adopted the Universal Declaration of Human Rights. Arising directly from the experiences of the Second World War, it was the first global expression of the innate rights afforded to all human beings. It reaffirmed the fundamental dignity and worth of the "human person" and promoted "universal respect for, and observance of, human rights and fundamental freedoms for all without distinction as to race, sex, language, or religion."

The Seven Year Dress

About the Author

Paulette Mahurin lives with her husband Terry and two dogs, Max and Bella, in Ventura County, California. She grew up in West Los Angeles and attended UCLA, where she received a Master's Degree in Science.

While in college, she won awards and was published for her short-story writing. One of these stories, *Something Wonderful,* was based on the couple presented in *His Name Was Ben*, which she expanded into a fictionalized novel in 2014. Her first novel, *The Persecution of Mildred Dunlap,* made it to Amazon bestseller lists and won multiple awards, including best historical fiction of the year 2012 in *Turning the Pages Magazine.* Her third novel, *To Live Out Loud,* won international critical acclaim and was recognized on multiple websites as a favorite-read book of 2015.

Semi-retired, she continues to work part-time as a Nurse Practitioner in Ventura County. When she's not writing, she does pro-bono consultation work with women with cancer, works in the Westminster Free Clinic as a volunteer provider, volunteers as a mediator in the Ventura County Courthouse for small claims cases, and involves herself, along with her husband, in dog rescue.

Profits from her book sales go to help rescue dogs from kill shelters.

Made in the USA
Middletown, DE
29 October 2018